MAN FROM
THE NORTH

LEE BEZOTTE

INSPARKET
— MEDIA —

Man from the North
Copyright © 2018 by Lee Bezotte All rights reserved.
First Print Edition: June 2018

Printed in the United States of America

Insparket Media
P.O. Box 1654
Moline, IL 61266

www.insparket.com

ISBN: 978-0-9976915-2-8
eISBN: 978-0-9976915-3-5

This book is dedicated to all who have tried hard to do the right thing and lived with the consequences.

CHAPTER ONE
DEATH MARCH

D ULNEAR USED HIS BARE HANDS to tear into the freshly cooked rabbit. He didn't have much of an appetite, but he needed to keep his strength up, so he ate anyway. As he did, his thoughts brought him back to many months ago when he fought for his life against the fellow northerner called Tromdel. Though the man was a violent blowhard with a thirst for conflict, he still regretted killing him. He could still hear the clashing of their swords, could smell the sweat and blood, and could still feel the sensation of plunging his sword into the chest of his opponent, forcing the life out of his large, muscular body.

He was haunted by what-ifs. What if he had not killed Tromdel? What if he had never left his home in the north in the first place? All he ever wanted was to escape the violence and hatred of his homeland, but now he had to return there to keep safe those who had become family to him: the kind-hearted boy Son and the quirky little girl Maren. It had only been a few days since he'd said goodbye to them, but he missed them so.

Dulnear was a warrior of the highest order. He was

taller, stronger, and more skilled in battle than anyone living in southern Aun. He enjoyed war, and never hesitated to slay anyone who dared to challenge him. But after leaving Tuas-arum, he'd discovered a new way to live. He found that he had a heart, and now that heart was breaking with each step closer to the northern border.

The howling of wolves in the darkness shook the man from his rumination. He didn't know how long he had been sitting there but his meal was now cold, and the fire had died down to a few lingering flames. He quickly ate the remainder of the roast rabbit and added more wood to the fire. He also added grass and leaves to cause it to smoke as much as possible. He knew that fire and smoke were the keys to staying alive when wolves were nearby.

Dulnear kept his back to the smoky blaze so the beasts would be unable to attack him from behind. He withdrew a dagger from his stash of blades of various sizes and sat with a keen ear for any movement in the blackness that surrounded him. With no stars or moonlight, it was impossible to see anything beyond the light his campfire provided. He knew he wouldn't be getting much sleep that night, and though he felt his life was as good as over, he had to stay alive until he reached Tuas-arum.

The next morning, Dulnear woke from what could hardly be called sleep. His vision was blurry, and his long fur coat felt heavier than usual. There was a silky haze across the ground that reached almost as high as he was tall. For a moment, he couldn't tell if he was awake or dreaming, but the dull ache in his chest confirmed he was indeed awake.

Though he was exhausted, he diligently followed his morning routine. He made coffee, read from an old book, and nibbled on whatever rations he had with him. The habit made him feel somewhat normal, despite the unusually bitter circumstance he found himself in.

When he was finished with the meager breakfast, the warrior from the north covered the smoldering embers of his campfire, collected his things, and moved toward the road, with each footstep feeling heavier than the last. As he journeyed, he noticed the haze lifting and he could see more clearly into the direction he was headed.

The land of Aun never did see much in the way of sunlight. The sky was a perpetual gray-white that stretched as far as one could see, and the melancholy air seemed to match Dulnear's mood as he continued on.

The road he traveled began to slope gradually to the north, and he could see a great distance. Either side of the road was blanketed with tall, lush grass stretched out over vacant fields, punctuated occasionally by derelict buildings and crumbling stone walls. In the distance, he could see the ruins of a large monastery. Old, abandoned holy places were common along the road he was walking, and the sight of them brought him a small amount of comfort amidst his deep sorrow, for they had a way of drawing him to the Unchanging One.

As Dulnear approached the place, he could see that there was very little left of the old structure besides the tall exterior rocky walls. They were gray and covered with moss, reaching skyward, with no roof to connect them. The man was almost certain that a forceful gust of wind would be sufficient to send them tumbling to the ground.

He left the road and walked out into the field where the ruins were situated. He stood in the large, ornate arched doorway and looked inside. Most of the mortar and rock that once rested inside the structure had been removed by nearby farmers to use for making the walls that surrounded their properties. As he surveyed the monastery, he said a prayer.

Dulnear asked the Great Father to relieve his heartache—but there was no relief. He prayed for words of comfort and wisdom—but none came. There was only silence and the faint whistle of the breeze blowing through the ruins, and the gentle sound of a cold, light rain that had begun to fall. He did everything he thought would please the Great Father, yet was weighed down by the greatest sadness he'd ever known.

Still, he lingered in the holy ruins for a while longer, walking around the outside of the crumbled cathedral. As he did, he touched the ancient walls and imagined what the old monks would have thought of his predicament. *I would bet that none of them had ever run a man through*, he thought to himself. He eventually came upon a cairstos flower growing out from a crack in the stone wall. He stared at the small blossom for a moment, admiring its ability to bloom without soil or very much sunlight. It reminded him of the boy he'd left in Laor, and he gently pulled it from the wall and placed it in his pocket.

When the rain became heavier and more persistent, the man from the north took shelter under a small doorway toward the back of the cathedral. He waited there, staring out into the field behind the structure until the rain subsided. Sighing, he made his way back to the road.

CHAPTER TWO
STIRRING TROUBLE

DULNEAR CONTINUED HIS LONG WALK north. He had reached one of the many villages that were scattered just past the outskirts of Ahmcathare, the largest city in Aun. From there, he could just barely make out some of the large spires and towers that dominated the distant city's skyline. Like giant, slender fingers, they reached skyward until they disappeared into the distant haze. He had no interest in visiting such a busy, teeming place, preferring the small communities and countryside. At least there he felt he had more room to move about without bumping into others in congested shops and streets. He had a particular disdain for large crowds, as they often made him irritable and tired. The village, by contrast, contained most of its buildings along a wide main street with ample room for carriages and people alike to move about with little crowding or frustration.

As he walked into the village, a funeral march was slowly moving down the road in his direction. The painted wagon carrying the coffin was driven by a weary-looking man dressed in black, with a tall hat that pressed his eyebrows into an angry expression. Alongside him sat a weeping woman with a veiled face, and walking behind the wagon was group of mourners following them to the cemetery.

The man from the north stepped to the side of the road as the company passed and lowered his head in respect. As he did, he thought about the day his lifeless body would be prepared for burial. It was very reasonable to believe that his own life would be over soon, and he wondered if anyone would mourn the passing of one who had ended the lives of so many others. Other than the children he'd left in Laor he had no family, no friends, and no real legacy. Like many northerners, he was a warrior, and most warriors receive their glory from victories, not from dying.

"Ye here for the funeral?" an elderly voice asked from nearby.

Dulnear raised his head to see an old gentleman standing next to him on the side of the road. "Just passing through. Are you?" he answered.

"Aye. Going to follow behind the other mourners once I catch my breath," the man said. He wore a threadbare suit and farmer's boots covered in mud. "I can't walk the long distances I used to," he added with a flagging exhale.

"My sympathy," the warrior said. "Was it a family member?"

The elderly man shook his head and, when he did, wispy white hair was pressed against his forehead by the wind. "Oh no," he said. "It was one of our village officials. He was very well-respected. Unfortunately, sickness got him, and he had to leave us early."

"I am sorry to hear that," Dulnear said. He wasn't very good at offering condolences but was sincere nonetheless.

"Such things happen," the old man said. "Sometimes it's better not to try and make sense of them."

The words of the elderly mourner didn't agree with the man from the north, who often tried to make sense of just about every experience, but he smiled and nodded anyway. When the man walked off to follow the processional, Dulnear noticed that there was a large inn just down the road. For several days he had slept very little. He had also eaten nothing but what he could forage for or catch along the road. He was exhausted and hungry, and thought that a hearty meal and a mattress might do him some good. He had a long walk ahead of him, and he needed the rest and nourishment.

Attached to the inn was a tavern and, after securing a room for the evening, Dulnear went in for dinner. He had been in many places like this; loud, untidy, and reeking of smoke and spilled beer. There was a long counter along the wall to his left with a handful of men standing next to it as they chatted and drank an early evening ale. Since most people were intimidated by the warrior's size and demeanor, they left him alone, which suited the man just fine. But there was something about this place that made him feel uneasy.

He ignored the feeling and found an available table at which to sit. It was towards the back corner of the tavern, and from there he could see most of the establishment, including the door. The man never sat with his back towards a door. It was a habit he'd developed living in the north, and one that had saved his life on many occasions.

As Dulnear sat and surveyed the room, he noticed an attractive, yet haggard-looking, barmaid rushing from table to table delivering full mugs of ale. He was impressed by her ability to carry five or six mugs at a time without spilling a drop. However, each time she came and went from behind the bar, she encountered the group of men standing there, and they were doling out obscene comments, arrogantly chuckling and grinning as if she were the object of a lewd joke.

When the barmaid arrived at Dulnear's table, he noticed that she was even more attractive, and more haggard-looking, now that she was close to him. There was something about her that made him feel relaxed. Before she could ask for his order he asked, "What is your name?"

The barmaid looked as if someone had just asked her the most absurd question ever, then composed herself and answered, "Faymia."

"Well, Faymia," he began, "I would like you to bring me the biggest bowl of lamb stew you have, and a mug of ale."

Faymia gave a frazzled yet courteous, "Yes, sir," and headed back to the kitchen for the stew. As she did, the man from the north watched the group of men that had been harassing her. They wore formal business clothing but carried themselves less like proper businessmen and more like trashy good-for-nothings. They were boisterous, had an over-inflated confidence, and an air of superiority. In addition, the scented musk they wore could be smelled from where Dulnear was seated. It didn't take long for him to deduce who the men were.

Slavers, the large warrior thought to himself. *They are the lowest of the low*.

It was illegal to capture slaves in Aun, but it was lawful to sell someone into slavery if they went willingly. That's what made the slavers so devious. They would move into a town and throw the grandest parties, many lasting for weeks or even months. Night after night, the townspeople would come and feast on rich foods, drink, and entertainment, all provided by the slavers. This would go on until the partygoers came to expect it, crave it, and refuse to live without it.

That's when the slavers began to make the people pay to continue their feasting. By then, the people were hooked on amusements and full stomachs, and every time the price to continue grew dearer, they willingly paid it until they had nothing left but their lives, and their lives they willingly gave to slavery in exchange for the promise of more food and more entertainment.

When Faymia returned to the table with the bowl of lamb stew Dulnear thanked her, but the warmth he carried earlier was gone. He now surmised that she was a slave, and he thought very little of anyone who would sacrifice so much for merrymaking and a full stomach. She set the stew on the table and went to the bar to retrieve his mug of ale.

When the barmaid came out from behind the bar with the tankard of brew, her way was blocked by the inebriated slavers. In addition to the usual vulgar remarks and laughter, the man who appeared to be the leader of the unwholesome group took the ale from her and began to drink it.

Fed up, hungry, and especially thirsty, Dulnear did not possess the patience to watch any longer. He stood up from the table, picked up his large bowl of lamb stew, and walked over to the group of musky-smelling drunkards.

In his long fur coat, with the hilt of an impressively large sword peeking out, the man from the north stood next to the barmaid and stared menacingly at the slavers while he scooped large spoonfuls of stew into his mouth.

The leader of the group, looking amused by Dulnear's presence, asked, "What's your problem, enormous goat? Did you lose your groomer?"

"I am thirsty, and you are delaying my ale," the man from the north answered as he took another mouthful of lamb and vegetables from his bowl.

A condescending grin crossed the slaver's face, slightly buried by his black, well-groomed mustache and beard. He bowed in mock respect, swept the oily black hair off of his forehead, and replied, "My apologies, you may have the rest of it." He then extended the half-empty mug towards the warrior.

Dulnear's expression remained stone-like, but he could feel his neck stiffen as the slavers chuckled at his expense. "I care not for the humor of slack-jawed ne'er-do-wells," he said. "Make it right."

The slaver chortled, then said, "As you wish," as he poured the remaining ale out on the floor in front of him.

As the man stood there smugly, waiting for a response, Dulnear quickly considered his possible actions, and the consequences those actions could bring. In his tired, thirsty, irritable state, he reckoned that he was going to be dead soon anyway, so there was no use defusing the situation. Besides, it had been a while since he had been in a good fight, and one might help to lighten his mood. He took the bowl of lamb stew he was holding and flung its contents onto the slaver, covering his head and shoulders with broth and vegetables.

Faymia gasped and slipped behind the bar while the five slavers accompanying their now stew-drenched friend froze. No longer smiling, the man brushed bits of meat and carrots off of his shoulders and spat, "Do you know who I am?"

"I care not," Dulnear answered curtly with nostrils flared.

"I am Tcharron of Daorcathare," the man boasted, keeping his eyes locked on Dulnear's.

"Who?" the man from the north replied with an unchanged face.

One of the accompanying slavers chimed in, "He's the richest slaver in southern Aun."

"I have never heard of you, nor am I impressed," the northerner said, keeping his stony disposition.

"Well, perhaps this would help us get acquainted," the man hissed as he withdrew a dagger from the inside of his vest. His friends followed suit and closed their circle around Dulnear.

For a moment, the man from the north stood as still as a statue. He took a deep, silent breath and held it for a moment as his mind nimbly designed an attack. He started moving with lightning speed. Before the slavers had a chance to react, he sent the soup bowl spinning at the head of the man nearest to him. The bowl ricocheted off the man's head, hitting the man closest to him, knocking both of them to the floor, clutching their skulls. Next, he hurled his spoon at the man on his left, lodging it into the soft flesh between the slaver's chest and shoulder. The man dropped to his knees, crying in agony as he attempted to pry the eating utensil from his body.

Tcharron raised his dagger but before he had a chance to strike, Dulnear punched him squarely in the chest, sending him flying into the two men behind him.

With all six men on the floor, the sizable brawler looked over them. He was disappointed by both the lack of wisdom in his actions and the brevity of the fight. He peered over the bar at a trembling Faymia, placed a coin upon it, and said, "I am sorry for the mess."

"It's okay," she replied through trembling lips, and reached up to take the coin.

Dulnear returned to the table to collect his bag, took a final look at his fallen opponents, and walked out the door as onlookers stared with mouths agape.

It was early evening when Dulnear returned to his room at the inn. There was still a trace of gray light coming through the large window and, since he was on the second floor, he could see lanterns being lit up and down the street as shopkeepers began shuttering their stores.

There was no need for him to light a lamp this evening. The fatigue of the last several days weighed on him like a heavy blanket, and his plan was to go straight to sleep. The large traveler looked at the bed and knew immediately that he would not fit on it, so he placed the mattress and bedding on the floor under the window, leaning the bed's wooden frame against the wall. Since all of the blankets were being used to supplement the inadequate mattress, he decided to leave his coat on.

Laying down with his coat wasn't the most comfortable thing, since there were several weapons stored underneath, but he was too tired to care. As he laid there, he felt his body sigh with relief. It was the most comfortable he'd been since he'd left Laor. Out of habit, he rested his hand on the hilt of his sword, occasionally swiping his thumb across the pommel.

Normally the man had the enviable ability to fall asleep quickly in any setting, but thoughts of his friends, Son and Maren, kept him awake. He had changed so much during his time with them, and he wondered what kind of impression his fight in the tavern would have made on their young hearts. He was glad they were not there to see it.

Eventually, the weariness from walking many miles, and the poor rest he had experienced for the last several nights, pulled him into sleep. As he slept, he dreamed that he was in battle, not with unskilled drunkards but experienced men of war. He fought with passion, as he sensed the battle was for something far bigger than foolish skirmishes or personal pride. A feeling of both dread and purpose filled him as he swung his sword without mercy or hesitation at his enemies. It was the type of battle a true northerner wished for but seldom experienced.

Suddenly, the door of the room was shattered, and men with weapons were pouring in like water from a broken dam. In the blink of an eye, Dulnear was awake, alert, and brandishing his enormous sword. He couldn't clearly see who they were, but he could smell Tcharron's scented musk.

The man from the north swung his sword into the darkness, striking an attacker. He heard a yell and the thud of a weapon hitting the ground. At almost the same time he felt something strike the side of his head, causing his ear to ring loudly. Urgently focusing his thoughts, he quickly reached behind and grabbed the mattress off the floor. With his left hand, he used the mattress like a shield to cover his head and shoulder, and with his right hand, he held out his sword like a javelin. He took a deep breath, clenched his jaw, and ran forward with all of his might, pushing and cutting through men until he slammed them into the adjacent wall. He could hear bones break and groans of pain but was compelled to flee as quickly as possible.

Before his attackers had a chance to strike a second blow, Dulnear dislodged his sword from the wall, ran back toward the window and crashed through it, leaping down onto the street below. Annoyed for having his sleep interrupted, and angry with himself for staying nearby after the incident in the bar, he ran off into the night.

CHAPTER THREE
RUNAWAY

ULNEAR SAT ON THE GROUND near his campfire. It was dark, and the earth was cold and hard, much like it always was. He was a few days' walk north of Ahmcathare and happy to have the incident with the slavers behind him. The clearing he sat in was surrounded by tall pine trees, which became more plentiful the further north he traveled. There were fewer farms and villages along the road, and that suited him just fine. Fewer villages meant less people, and less people meant less chances for confrontation.

He sat staring into the fire, listening to the evening breeze, lost in thought. As he poked at the flames with a stick, he heard the gentle sound of a snapping twig from behind a nearby tree. Instinctively, he put his hand inside his coat and reached for a dagger. Gripping his weapon he sat motionless, waiting, willing his heartbeat to remain calm as he listened.

Several seconds went by and there was no other noise. He tossed a pebble in the direction of the sound but there was only silence. This only increased the man's concern, since an animal surely would have run away from the pebble. Finally, he yelled with an intimidating voice, "Come out of there!"

Still not a sound. Convinced he was not alone, he yelled again, "Come out of there or meet my sword!" and he flung his dagger at the tree, embedding it in the trunk.

There was a gasp in the darkness, and then the sound of footsteps scurrying away. Dulnear jumped to his feet and ran toward the noise. Away from the fire, the woods were as black as coal. Rather than giving chase, he stopped and retrieved his dagger, then stood there, listening and waiting.

First, there was the sound of running. Then, there was the sound of a body colliding with a tree. The man from the north shook his head and grinned as he imagined what it must have looked like. Led by the person's heavy, pained breathing, it was easy for the warrior to locate them, grab them by the leg, and drag them back to his campfire.

"Why are you following me?" the man from the north growled as he dragged the soul closer to the fire.

"Please don't hurt me!" the figure pleaded, with arms flailing.

Dulnear, surprised at recognizing the voice, let go of the person's leg. It was the barmaid from Ahmcathare. By the flickering firelight he could see that she was dressed in men's clothing and her dark-brown hair was pulled back into a braid. "Faymia?"

"Y-you remember my name?" she asked, still frightened.

The warrior stood there silently, pondering the situation.

"I'm sorry for following you," she whimpered. "I had nowhere else to turn."

Not satisfied with the incompleteness of her answer, he repeated his question. "Again, why are you following me?"

Faymia swallowed and answered, "When my master assembled his men to attack you in your room, I escaped. I stole these clothes and ran, and when I saw you jump down onto the street, I followed you. I thought since you fought the slavers in the pub, you would protect me."

"I had merely reached my limit for barroom idiocy. It had nothing to do with you," Dulnear explained coldly. "You are a slave. You chose to forfeit proper treatment for a full belly."

Faymia slowly stood to her feet. Her eyes looked as if she had just received a blow to the stomach, but her posture displayed something more stern. Though she was much smaller than the man from the north, she breathed deeply, drew her shoulders back, and declared, "I'm not proud of my mistakes. I've made many, but that doesn't make you better than me!"

Dulnear raised his chin slightly, crossed his arms, and retorted, "Absolutely I am better than you! I am a warrior of the highest degree, I was born of one of the greatest clans in Tuas-arum, I have tamed both man and beast, and I would NEVER exchange my freedom for the promise of another custard pie!"

The woman's display of backbone didn't last long. Her shoulders slumped, her hands trembled and she looked away, staring into the night as if she hoped something would come out of the dark forest to make her life better.

An argument was happening inside the mind of the

warrior from the north. He had a genuine disdain for slaves and their masters, but he could see how his words had wounded Faymia, and he no longer wished to be a person who wounded others. After standing there silently for a while, he rubbed the back of his neck, pointed to the side of the fire that was opposite his belongings, and offered, "You may sleep there for the night. The accommodations are not much. I will have to decide what to do with you in the morning."

Faymia looked at the ground that Dulnear pointed to. Like the rest of the area, it was covered in only dirt and pine needles. Without looking at her reluctant host, she walked to the other side of the fire and laid down. She had no blanket or bedding, only the clothes she wore.

The man from the north watched the woman carefully. He then returned to his things and laid down himself. He used his bag as a pillow and stared into the blackness above the trees. It felt strange for him to have a woman sharing his camp with him, even if she was a slave. The harsh words he spoke were nagging at him, and he didn't want them to be the final words he spoke that day. He broke the silence. "Excuse me, but I must compliment you. I am not easily followed."

There was no reply.

"And my name is Dulnear," he added.

Still no reply.

The warrior sighed, closed his eyes, and tried to will himself to sleep.

Faymia shivered as she laid curled up on the cold, hard ground. Her head was swirling with thoughts about her decision to escape the slavers. She knew that she had taken a considerable risk but had little to lose, and longed to be free once again.

There was something about the way the man from the north carried himself in the tavern that made her trust him. It may have just been that it was the first time anyone had dared to interrupt when she was being harassed. Now that she was out in the woods alone with him, she wasn't so sure she'd judged his character correctly, especially after his less-than-hospitable reception.

His words pierced her and she felt ashamed. She knew he was right about slaves, but wished with everything in her that it didn't hurt so much to hear the truth. Her back was toward the fire, and she hoped he wasn't looking at her. The dread that she had made a terrible mistake by following him was growing, and she felt as if the ground was slowly sinking beneath her. She couldn't go back; she had no family or friends to turn to, and the person she wished would keep her safe seemed exasperated by her presence. Her life felt like one bad choice after another, leaving her cold and hungry, and on the ground with a grumpy, overgrown swordsman.

The woman wondered if Tcharron was looking for her. She had been gone for a few days now and had seen no sign of him or any of his companions. She did, however, have a haunting fear that she would wake up one morning to see slavers surrounding her to take her back.

This night was different though. There was a warrior nearby, and he would not be taken by surprise. She believed that, no matter how he felt about her, he hated the slavers so much that he would fight them if they ever came around, and that gave her a small amount of comfort. It was that bit of comfort that she held on to.

Eventually, her thoughts turned toward the years she'd lived before becoming a slave. The freedom she held then, she took for granted, not knowing what she had. As a girl, she often pined for greener pastures, more luxuries, and a more permissive mother. Looking back, she found it ridiculous that she ever felt restrained as a free person, and would give anything for just a taste of those days once again.

She reflected on these things until her tired eyes could no longer stay open. She closed them, curled up a little more tightly, and drifted into a restless sleep.

The next morning was strangely still and drenched in mist. There was neither the sound of birds singing nor a breeze through the trees. Dulnear sat up and stirred the glowing embers into a small fire that he could make his coffee over. As he did, he noticed that Faymia was gone from her sleeping place, and no longer in the clearing. *Just as well*, he thought to himself as a sense of relief began to rise in his chest. *Where I am going is no place for a woman like her, and I am no slave liberator.*

The man from the north nibbled on a cake made of grain and oil while he sipped his coffee. He was just about finished when Faymia came into the clearing with an armful of wild nuts and berries. He unconsciously let out a sigh when he realized that he was not going to be alone after all.

When the woman sat down, she gestured toward the

food that she had foraged, but Dulnear shook his head no. He refused to take any action that he believed would place him in debt to a slave.

As she sat nervously filling her stomach, Dulnear observed her oversized boots and coat, and wondered who she stole them from. He then looked up to see purple and yellow bruises around her mouth and right eye. He had not noticed them in the dark the night before. His eyes narrowed, and he used a gentle tone to ask, "Did Tcharron do that to you?"

Still struggling to look Dulnear in the eyes, Faymia wiped the berry juice from her hands onto the ground and answered, "No, Tcharron fancies himself too good for that sort of thing. He has hired lackeys do his beating for him." She then examined her hands for lingering stains and rubbed them on her oversized pant legs.

Still struggling to find the right words for the situation, the man from the north asked, "Why would he do such a thing?"

Finally looking him in the eyes, the barmaid nervously wrung her hands and answered, "They beat me because of what you did."

Dulnear felt as if he had been hit with an anvil. His hands began to tremble, and the forest seemed to spin around him. He dropped his coffee cup to the ground and said, "But what I did to Tcharron had nothing to do with you."

"That's not the way he saw it," Faymia explained. "You interrupted him while he was harassing me. In his twisted way of thinking, it was my fault that you injured him and his men." She then paused and added, "Slaves are

21

very convenient when looking for a person on which to place the blame. We are not allowed to argue our defense."

"I am so sorry," was all the warrior could manage to say, though he wanted to say more. The weight of the realization of what his actions cost the barmaid caused him to lower his head, hiding his eyes from her as he stared into the waning fire.

"It's okay," she whispered. "I know you didn't mean for it to happen."

Dulnear raised his head and looked at Faymia's bruised face. "I am returning to the north," he said. "I do not know what awaits me there, and I am sure it will not be pleasant. You may accompany me as far as the Fuar River, but I must go on from there alone."

A look of relief washed over the woman and she walked over to the remorseful warrior and hugged his neck. "Thank you," she said. "I promise not to be a burden."

The man from the north wiped a tear from his eye. He felt awkward that a strange woman was hugging him, but relieved that she didn't hold his actions against him. He took a deep breath, gathered his things, stood up and said, "I will do my best to protect you while we travel. However, I would suggest that you give thought to what you will do when we reach the Fuar."

"I will," Faymia promised. "And again, thank you."

"You are welcome," Dulnear said as he clumsily patted her on the shoulder and gave her what he hoped was a reassuring smile, though he wasn't sure. Then he put out the fire and said, "If you are ready, let us head toward the road."

CHAPTER FOUR

ALONG THE BRINK ROAD

ULNEAR AND FAYMIA CONTINUED ALONG the road leading north. After a couple of days' travel, they came to a small hamlet with a pub and a few modest shops. Since they were closer to the northern border, the tall warrior did not experience the usual stares and strange looks he was used to receiving in other parts of Aun.

Faymia, on the other hand, was looked at quite oddly in her oversized man's outfit. Noticing the attention the woman was getting, Dulnear suggested, "I think it might be time to find you clothing more suitable for travel. It will be easier on your feet, and you can use your hands for something other than holding up your trousers."

"But I have no money," the woman admitted hesitantly.

"I will take care of it," Dulnear responded with an amiable expression.

Looking slightly embarrassed, the woman asked, "Are you sure? I don't want to put you out."

"Not at all," the man from the north said. "It is the least I can do." He still felt the weight of causing Faymia pain, and the more time he spent with her, the less he saw her as a slave and the more he considered her an acquaintance.

The two of them entered a small textile and clothing shop. Dulnear followed her to the only aisle of clothing that would be suitable for a woman to travel and camp in. As he stood there watching her look for pants and a shirt that would fit, he felt ill at ease. He had never spent this much time with a woman before, and watching one shop for clothing was something completely foreign to him.

Faymia unfolded a shirt and held it to herself. She turned around toward Dulnear and asked, "What do you think of this one?"

It was a plain white shirt, and the awkward feeling the man from the north already felt multiplied many times over with the question. He answered, "I do not...um, I mean, it is grand. I will meet you over there," and found himself backing out of the aisle to give the woman space to discover what she'd like to wear on her own.

He waited for quite some time by the counter, where the shop owner tried to make small talk with him. "From the north, are ye?" he asked through a bushy brown mustache.

"Yes," Dulnear answered plainly.

The shopkeeper wore an odd expression. "Are ye headed there now?"

"Yes," the man from the north said.

The store owner narrowed his eyes and asked, "Is the woman going with ye?"

Dulnear was in no mood for conversation with the man, and didn't want to let on that his companion was a slave. "She is an old friend from these parts," he answered curtly.

"Oh? Where exactly?" the man pressed.

The northern warrior's patience was beginning to run thin. His nostrils flared and his temples tightened. He glared at the man behind the counter and snarled, "You will have to forgive me, but I am not in the mood for conversation."

The lanky shopkeeper's eyes grew large and he swallowed. "I didn't mean to be rude," he said. "It's been a slow day, and there 'aven't been many people to talk to."

"Well you will have to save it for your next customer," Dulnear said as he crossed his arms.

"As you wish, sir," the man said. "My apologies."

When Faymia finally came out to join the man from the north, she was dressed in a pair of pants with the shirt she'd shown Dulnear earlier. She also had on a green tunic, tall boots, and a long, gray hooded cloak that could double as a blanket. In addition, she had picked out a bag, a canteen, and a few other small items to make life on the road easier.

When the warrior saw her, he suppressed a smile from appearing at the corner of his mouth. Gone was the harried barmaid in oversized men's clothing. She now looked like a proper traveler, and much happier in clothing that fit the way it was intended. As he paid for her new belongings, he exchanged an unpleasant glance with the shopkeeper. The warrior and Faymia then left the shop together.

"Now let us have a good meal," the man from the north suggested, shaking off the conversation with the store owner.

Faymia said nothing, but smiled as she kept pace with the man's long, deliberate stride.

As they walked across the street to the pub, there were far fewer strange looks from the villagers; only the occasional glances that are common when one recognizes that someone is not native to the area. Though the air was cool, Dulnear chose to sit at one of the three tables situated outside of the pub instead of going in.

It wasn't long before the owner of the small tavern came out to greet the two travelers. He was portly and rosy-cheeked, and his hair looked as if it had been blown in every direction by the wind. "You're welcome. Why don't ye come inside, where it's warmer?" he asked.

Not really considering how Faymia felt, Dulnear answered, "We are fine here, but we are hungry." After his last experience on the inside of a pub, he simply wanted to have his meal where he could eat it in peace and leave without any hinderances.

"Then ye've come to the right place," the man replied. "I've just pulled a roast out of the oven and have plenty of veg."

"That sounds perfect. Two portions, please," the hungry warrior ordered. "And two mugs of ale."

The friendly proprietor went back inside, leaving Dulnear and Faymia alone at their table. It was the first time the two had ever sat together without the need to perform camp duties. There was nothing to gather, nothing to cook, and nothing to clean. The brief moment of simply facing each other brought back the awkward feelings the man from the north felt in the store, but with greater intensity.

Faymia broke the silence. "Thank you for these

clothes, and the bag and canteen," she said with genuine appreciation.

Relieved that he didn't have to initiate their conversation, Dulnear answered, "It is my pleasure. They are fine garments and should serve you well." He noticed how the cloak draped over her slender shoulders and, for the first time, how her silver eyes and raven hair contrasted her smooth, fair skin. "You look very nice," he added. "In the new clothes, that is. That stolen slaver's suit was not very becoming."

Faymia smiled slightly. "No, I suppose it wasn't," she admitted. "And traveling would be difficult in my barmaid's clothes."

"And the bruises are almost completely healed," Dulnear added.

The woman looked down and adjusted her new tunic. She then rubbed her forearms and said, "Thank you."

Dulnear wasn't sure why the statement made his companion feel uncomfortable, but he made a mental note to not mention the bruises again. "I am very hungry. How about you?" he asked, changing the subject.

"Yes, me too," she answered, turning her gaze back toward him.

Just then, the pub owner returned with two plates of roast lamb and vegetables piled high, and two mugs of ale. "Now, I'll be inside if you need anything else. Enjoy!" he announced, and disappeared back into the tavern.

The two sat for quite some time, enjoying their meal together and each other's company. Conversation was sparse, but Dulnear felt a lift in the heaviness for the first time since leaving Laor. There was something about his new companion's unassuming demeanor and gentle temperament that was slowly growing on him.

After they had eaten their fill, Dulnear and Faymia continued their walk north. Now that they were only a day or two from the Fuar River, the man from the north felt a tightening in his chest. He did not want to lose the companionship the slave woman brought, but knew that bringing her to Tuas-arum would only add to her pain. The heaviness that had lifted during their meal together was returning in force. "Have you thought about what you will do when we reach the Fuar?" he asked.

"I don't know," the woman answered honestly. "My mother was my only family and she passed on years ago. If I stay in one place too long, Tcharron is sure to find me. I suppose I will keep moving until a solution presents itself."

The man from the north furrowed his brow and asked, "Do you have any friends who can help you?"

"I'm afraid the few friends I had became slaves at the same time I did. I don't know what has become of them," she answered as she looked down at the ground in front of her.

A hint of the familiar disdain for slaves returned to the man from the north. He could not understand how one could so easily give up their freedom. "How long ago did you enter into slavery?" he asked.

"About five seasons ago," she answered. "The slavers came to my village shortly after my mother died. It was such a difficult time for me. She was my only family. I felt abandoned and lonely, and when someone came to my village offering a distraction from what I was going through, I was happy to partake."

A measure of understanding settled on the man from the north. He continued questioning as they walked together. "How long did the slavers stay in your village?"

Faymia looked toward the sky, recalling the days of feasting and entertainment. "Many weeks. Going to their nightly amusements became a part of my life, even after they started to make us pay for all of the festivities." She then looked back down at the road, swallowed, and kept her head turned so that it was difficult for Dulnear to see her eyes.

"Did you lose much during that time?" he asked, though he was sure he knew the answer.

Faymia's voice started to tremble. "Everything. I sold family heirlooms to keep feasting. I even sold our land. When everything was gone, I offered the slavers my body, which they gladly took." Tears fell from the woman's eyes as she recounted, "I felt so ashamed. When they wouldn't accept a night in bed with me anymore, I chose slavery. I believed that, since I had nothing of value anymore, there was no point in trying to live free." She then used the end of her sleeve to wipe her pink nose as she took a deep breath.

"Is that when they put you to work in the pub?" Dulnear asked as a look of concern grew in his eyes.

"I only wish that is what happened," Faymia answered through her tears. She exhaled and lamented, "They put me right to work as a woman of the night. I was with many men until Tcharron felt I was used up and no longer desirable. That is when he put me to work in the pub."

She stopped walking and stood in the road, weeping. Her shoulders shook and she folded her arms, keeping one hand over her eyes.

The man from the north stopped and faced her. He was moved by her story but did not know how to comfort her, so he simply placed his hand on her shoulder as she trembled and cried. Faymia quickly threw her arms around the large man's trunk and sobbed into his fur coat.

Dulnear felt the desire to alleviate her sadness but had no idea how. He patted her on the back and whispered, "It is okay. Everything will be all right." They were words that he had little confidence in, but he said them with as much conviction that he could muster.

"I am like filthy rags now," the woman confided. "No virtuous man would ever want me after all I've done."

"It is okay," he said again, and he kept his arm around her until she regained her composure. When she did, he offered her a handkerchief, which she gladly accepted.

"I'm sorry," Faymia said. "I don't mean to blubber."

"It is okay," the man from the north repeated. Trying to think of a way to cheer her up, he quipped, "If you cannot share your feelings with a sword-wielding, giant man from the north, then who can you share them with?"

The woman giggled as she wiped her eyes with the handkerchief. "Thank you," she said before handing it back to Dulnear.

The man from the north held his hand up. "You can keep that," he said. "I have another."

Faymia smiled in appreciation as she placed the damp cloth in her pocket, and the two of them continued their march north.

The next morning, Dulnear awoke to the smell of a squirrel roasting over a fire. Faymia was tending the meat and, when she saw that the warrior was awake, she offered him some wild berries and a cup of coffee.

The man from the north sat up and looked around as many thoughts rushed to fill his mind. He normally would not have accepted generosity from a slave, but was softening toward this one. Also, he was always the first to rise and, though a hot breakfast was a pleasant surprise, he didn't like that he'd slept through Faymia's meal preparations. He was both disappointed in himself and impressed by the woman's ability to move about so without waking him. "What is the occasion?" he asked as he reached for the coffee.

"We should be reaching the Fuar today," she answered. "I thought it would be nice to share a full breakfast together before we parted ways." She then tore off a small section of the squirrel for herself and handed the rest to Dulnear.

"I see. Thank you," he answered as he sank his teeth into the meat. He then took a sip of the coffee and admitted, "I will miss having a traveling companion."

Faymia looked down and smiled. "I will miss traveling with you as well. Thank you for listening to my woes. I have not been able to share them with anyone for a very long time."

"It is my pleasure. I mean, I am glad I could offer you a listening ear," Dulnear assured.

The woman smiled and observed, "Perhaps you northerners aren't as cold and mean as the rumors say you are."

The man from the north chuckled and said, "I am afraid the rumors do not go far enough. We are far worse than they say."

"Then I'm glad I happened upon this northerner," Faymia said as she took a sip of her coffee.

Dulnear sat up and ate the rest of his portion of squirrel, taking time to savor each bite. He also sipped at his coffee, making no effort to hurry through his meal. The two of them enjoyed their breakfast together and their conversation was easy, discussing things like the nearby flora and the chill in the weather as of late.

When they were done eating, they gathered their things and headed back to the road. The man from the north walked a little slower than usual so Faymia wouldn't have to work so hard to keep up with him. He was not eager to reach the Fuar River, since it meant parting company. However, by late afternoon, they reached the Brink Road, the road running east and west along the river. It was bordered by grassy fields to the south and was thick with trees to the north. The distance between the road and the cliffs that bordered the southern edge of the river was a morning's walk and was covered in dense forest.

As they stood where the two roads met, the man from the north pointed out, "The river is just on the other side of the woods." He then looked at Faymia and confessed, "I am glad that we were able to travel together."

"As am I," the woman said with a sad expression. "It's been years since I've felt safe around anyone. Thank you for being such an honorable man."

Dulnear felt encouraged by her compliment. He asked, "Do you know where you will go from here?"

"West, I suppose, maybe all the way to the sea," she answered.

The tall warrior looked westward down the road. There was a nervousness growing in his chest. He looked down at his feet, swallowed, and said, "The Contuent Bridge is a couple days' walk west. It would be much safer for me to cross the river there."

Faymia bounced lightly on her toes and her eyebrows raised. "Well, I would be happy to accompany you to the bridge, if you'd like me to."

Dulnear's eyes smiled and a warmth filled his cheeks. There was something about knowing that he didn't have to say goodbye just yet that set him at ease. "Very well then," he said. "But we will definitely have to say goodbye at the bridge."

"I understand," she replied, and they walked east together along the Brink Road.

As the afternoon light began to fade, Dulnear decided it would be good to veer off of the north side of the road to find a place to camp for the night. They walked for a way into the woods until they found a small clearing among the pines. The ground was uneven and hard, but it would do.

"We'll stay here," he said as he unslung his bag from his shoulder and dropped it to the ground with a thud.

Faymia seemed to be at ease in a way the man from the north had never noticed before. She set her bag down as well. "Looks good to me!" she exclaimed, and began to collect sticks and twigs for a fire.

Dulnear interrupted her chore by saying, "Come for a short walk with me, I would like to show you something."

The woman set the wood down in the clearing and the two of them walked north through the trees until they reached a steep cliff overlooking the Fuar River. High above the river they could see across to the northern bank, which was a gradual slope covered in lush forest. It was much different from the tall cliffs of the southern bank they stood on.

"There is my homeland," Dulnear shared with mixed feelings. "Beyond the forest lies rolling hills that turn into majestic mountains." After a pause, he added, "'Tis a shame such a beautiful place has to be filled with such bitter, petty people."

"What are those?" Faymia asked as she pointed to a cluster of dark trees in the distance.

"They are the black pines," the warrior answered. "They have sharp needles as black as night, and they only grow in the north."

The woman stared across the river with a look of awe. "I'm glad you decided to cross at the Contuent," she said. "It looks awfully dangerous here."

"And cold," Dulnear added. "East of here, there are large rocks and a shallow bed. I have crossed there in the past; but here, the river is deep and wild." He then took a deep breath and inhaled the misty air rising from the rushing waters below.

Faymia looked at the warrior and asked, "What is your home like?"

"It is a fine estate nestled in the rolling hills of Tuas-arum," he said as he gazed into the northern horizon. He looked proud, and continued, "The largest oaks you have ever seen grow there, as big as a house and as strong as a boulder." Then, as the reality of his journey returned to his mind, his shoulders sank and he closed his eyes for a moment before looking at Faymia and suggesting, "I suppose we should make a fire before it gets too dark."

"Okay," she answered, and the two of them slowly headed back to the clearing.

After gathering more wood, building up the fire, and nibbling on some wild carrot, Dulnear situated himself on the ground to go to sleep for the night. On the other side of the fire, Faymia was curled up under her cloak, using her bag for a pillow. Without her awareness, he looked at her lying there one last time before laying his head down.

The powerful man gazed silently into the somber night sky. Now that he had stood and looked upon the north, a greater sense of angst and uncertainty was sinking into him. Temptation to run, and avoid making restitution, filled him. He imagined taking Faymia to Laor and reuniting with Son and Maren. He thought perhaps he could elude Tromdel's family and still have the life he wanted. It was a wish that seemed too good to ever be true.

While pondering these things, something else came over Dulnear. It was a feeling that something wasn't right. It was a feeling he experienced often, and had learned to pay heed to it, for it was seldom wrong. He exposed the hilt of his sword and rested his hand on the grip. He listened carefully, but could only hear the sound of the river in the distance, the crackling of the dying fire, and the heavy breathing of the woman sleeping nearby. It was a long time before he fell asleep and, when he did, his dreams were filled with blood and steel.

CHAPTER FIVE
BESIEGED

D ULNEAR SAT UP QUICKLY WITH his sword drawn. He sprang to his feet and tried to peer through the morning mist. Faymia was still sleeping, but he was convinced that he heard whispers, like ghosts in the woods.

The skilled warrior walked slowly and quietly past the southern edge of the clearing, straining to hear through the sounds of the nearby river and the morning songs of birds. *Perhaps I am hearing things*, he thought to himself. After surveying the area, he returned to the clearing. When he did, he felt his stomach sink and his temples tighten as he saw a man standing in the middle of his camp. He was restraining Faymia with one arm, and with the other, he held a dagger to her throat.

The man wore a ragged shirt that exposed his muscular arms. He was covered in soil, and a line of black paint ran down his face. He stood silently and expressionless with his blade ready to take the woman's life.

"What do you want?" the man from the north asked with curled lip and squinting eyes. He gripped the hilt of his sword tightly, and his mind began to design a quick and skilled execution of the strange man.

There was only eerie silence in response as the man stood so still that he hardly seemed to be breathing.

"WHAT DO YOU WANT?" he asked again, drawing his sword back as he took a step closer.

There was another whisper in the breeze and, from what seemed like nowhere, similar-looking men stepped into the clearing from all sides. They were brandishing knives and hatchets of various sizes. Dulnear swallowed and froze in his tracks.

"It's not wise to challenge the Malitae," said a voice from behind the northerner.

The familiar scent of musk filled Dulnear's nostrils. He looked over his shoulder and watched as Tcharron stepped into the clearing and stood between the man from the north and his captive friend.

"These are the warriors of the southern islands? I thought they served no master," Dulnear observed with disdain in his voice.

"Everyone has a price," the slaver replied. "And this woman still has some value to me."

"By the way you were treating her in the pub, I would have guessed she was worth nothing," the man from the north retorted.

"Let's just say that my reputation is important to me, and no one runs off without paying for it," Tcharron snorted arrogantly. He was then flanked by two other well-dressed slavers, one of them carrying shackles.

As the three men turned to place the shackles on Faymia, Dulnear raised his sword above his head. As he did, the mercenary holding onto the woman tightened his grip and she let out a muffled shriek. Just then three more

Malitae stepped in front of the man from the north. They each held weapons and took a fighting posture.

The hair on Dulnear's neck stood on end and he growled quietly as he locked eyes with the warrior who held Faymia.

"Don't make things worse, northerner!" Tcharron yelled. "I'm just here to collect my property, and these men are here to make sure you don't get in the way." He then rolled his eyes and condescendingly shook his head at Dulnear.

The tall northerner lowered his sword. With grit in his eyes, he stared at the slavers as they locked the irons onto his friend's hands and feet. "Very well then," he conceded. He knew that he was out-armed and out-manned. His only option was to wait for an opportunity to make a move.

The three slavers began to lead the woman out of the clearing while the warriors from the southern islands stayed in place. A sense of loss and injustice began to wrap itself around Dulnear. He clenched his jaw and once again thought, *I'm already a dead man*.

The man from the north slashed upward, cutting off the left arm of the Malitae warrior to his right. In a single motion he withdrew a second, smaller sword from inside his coat and used it to slash across the chest of the second warrior. He then cut down the third—but not before the man could plunge a knife into Dulnear's side.

The fur-clad man growled as he dropped his second sword, removed the knife from his side and threw it at the nearest slaver, lodging it in his back and dropping him to the ground. Tcharron and the surviving slaver threw Faymia to the ground and began running toward the road.

"Kill them both!" the slave master ordered as he ran to escape the northerner's wrath.

Blades of all shapes and sizes began to whoosh through the air. With incredible accuracy, Dulnear used his sword to keep many of them from striking him as he ran toward Faymia. He scooped her up and held her close, using himself and his heavy coat to shield her from the onslaught.

There was shouting in a language that was unfamiliar to the man from the north and, before he could fully stand with the woman in his arms, a man was attached to his back with a long knife. He dropped Faymia and reached back, but the southern warrior evaded his grasp and swiped at him with his blade. Noticing a tree just a couple paces behind him, Dulnear lurched backward, crushing the man against it.

As soon as the southern warrior dropped to the ground, Dulnear regathered his companion, turned north, and raced as fast as he could, picking up the sword he'd dropped along the way. Since his arms were being used to hold Faymia, he could only use his swords to guard his face and head as he lowered his shoulder and plowed through any Malitae that got in his way.

The warriors from the southern islands pursued him with frightening howls and skillfully aimed hatchets, several of them striking the man from the north, penetrating his heavy coat. Through the pain, and realization that he might not survive the day, he willed his body to keep moving at full speed. He had no other options, and he had to keep his friend alive.

Through the terrible chase, Dulnear could hear Faymia cry out, "Dulnear, the cliff!"

"Hold your breath, my friend," the man answered.

Weaving through trees like a hunted animal, staying only a few paces ahead of the bloodthirsty mercenaries, Dulnear reached the cliff over the Fuar River. He did not slow down or look over his shoulder. He ran hard and purposefully over the edge, plunging into the deep, wild, frigid waters below.

CHAPTER SIX
THE COLD FORCE

THE COLD WATER FELT LIKE thousands of needles penetrating Dulnear's skin. It was as if the water had a will, and its desire was to hold the man under. As the frigid Fuar carried him downstream, he shed his sword belt and coat while keeping his breath held. His sole focus was on getting himself and Faymia to the surface before the water forced its way into their lungs.

Like a rag doll, he was flung about by the wild, angry river. He held onto the woman's waist, hoping that her ribs would not break under the pressure. When he finally reached air, he did his best to keep her head above water while he desperately searched for something he could grab ahold of.

Out of the corner of his eye, he spotted a fallen pine tree extending from the north bank. With all of his strength, he maneuvered his body so that the current would carry him toward it. Just in time, he was able to grab the top of the tree before being rushed further downstream.

The weight of the two travelers almost caused the dead tree to dislodge from the bank, and the man from the north knew he had to make it to shore before that happened.

"Can you grab the tree?" the man asked his companion over the roaring of the Fuar.

There was no response. Faymia was completely limp. The warrior hadn't noticed before, since his limbs were numb from the cold. He hefted her onto the pine tree and began to make his way up its trunk. He made it to the shallows, stumbling over his own frozen feet. When he finally arrived at the shore, he dislodged the tree and carefully pulled it onto land, making sure Faymia stayed out of the water.

Dulnear dropped the log and ran to the woman. He had very little feeling in his arms and legs and it was a labor to use them as he dragged her further ashore. When he turned his friend over, he saw that her face was blue and she wasn't breathing. Panic and regret were quickly replacing the numbness as he prayed under his breath for her life.

"Faymia!" he called out. "Faymia!!"

There was no response.

Dulnear raised his friend's cold, wet form into a sitting position and began slapping her on the back. His heart beat faster, and a tightness in his chest accentuated his panic. "Faymia!" he called out again.

A gurgling cough emitted from the woman, with a modest amount of river water. The man from the north laid her back down, turned her on her side, and patted her on the back as gently as he could, considering the loss of feeling in his hands. When she began to cough some more, vomiting up the rest of the water, a feeling of relief washed over him.

"That is it," Dulnear encouraged. "Get it all out. Breathe slowly."

Faymia laid there, stunned. She started breathing quickly and aggressively, with eyes still closed. "Can't feel…" she said before her voice became too faint to hear.

"Hold on!" the warrior urged, and then ran to retrieve some dry wood.

Keeping one eye on his companion, he quickly built a fire a little further up the bank, away from the spray of the river. It was a difficult task to perform with numb hands, but he managed. When the flame no longer required his attention, he ran back to the woman and picked her up in both arms. "It is okay," he tried to reassure her, holding back a look of concern, and a tear. "I have you. It is going to be all right."

He carried her back to the fire and set her down close to it. She sat, hunched over, facing the heat, and began to shiver. With each passing moment, the shivering became more intense until she looked up helplessly at Dulnear.

The man from the north continued coaching, "Keep breathing. We need to get that cloak and that tunic off of you." Then, realizing that the woman still had chains on her ankles, he collected a couple of large river rocks and used them to fracture the chains and set her free.

Once free, Faymia's hands were trembling too violently to untie her cloak, so Dulnear knelt to help. His own clumsy, feeling-less hands weren't much better, but he managed. He took the cloak and tunic and hung them from a nearby tree to dry. When he returned, he sat down close to the woman, encouraging her to move closer to the fire.

As sensitivity began to return to the warrior's arms, he noticed that the numbness was being replaced by pain. He looked down and saw that his hands and forearms were covered in cuts and gashes of various sizes, and blood was now trickling down his arms. The temporary loss of feeling caused him to forget about the injuries he'd received from the Malitae. He had also received several scratches and scrapes from moving the tree and gathering wood.

"You're b-bleeding!" Faymia exclaimed through her shivers.

"It looks worse than it is," he assured her, and went to the river to rinse the blood from his arms. As he washed, he surveyed the southern cliffs for pursuing Malitae. Seeing no one, he thought that the river must have washed them further west than he originally believed.

When Dulnear returned to the fire, he sat down and asked, "How do you feel?"

Still shivering some, she answered, "N-n-never better."

Relieved by her playful answer, the man from the north smiled with his eyes and said, "Good. Let us take these boots off and dry your feet. We need to get you warm and dry as soon as possible."

"What about you?" Faymia replied.

"It is okay," he answered as he carefully removed the woman's boots. "I have been swimming in frigid waters since I was a boy."

"You're not even shivering," the woman observed.

"Not at all," he said as he set the boots by the fire. "It is the fingers and toes that get to me. They go numb in the cold water, and I get as clumsy as a bear wearing mittens."

"A bear wearing mittens?" the woman chuckled.

"Well, that would be a sight to see." She then paused for a moment and asked, "Are you sure you're going to be okay?"

It suddenly struck Dulnear that the sword he had been carrying since his coming-of-age ceremony was at the bottom of the Fuar, as well as all of his other weapons. His coat was gone too, and he'd left his bag of supplies at the campsite when he escaped the Malitae. All that he had was the clothes he was wearing and a hunting knife that was attached to his belt. A feeling of nakedness came over him. His sword and coat had been with him for as long as he could remember. He answered as confidently as he could, "I will be fine."

As the shivers subsided and feeling returned to her hands and feet, Faymia watched the man from the north as he stood near the river's edge, scanning the tops of the cliffs on the other side once again. The shirt he wore had no sleeves, and she couldn't help but notice the many scars on his arms and the blood that occasionally trickled from his fresh wounds.

She replayed the events of the morning many times in her mind, remembering how it felt to be held captive by the Malitae warrior, and the feeling of dread when she saw Tcharron. She also remembered how it felt when she was being whisked off under the protection of Dulnear. It was a new feeling and she couldn't quite identify it. No man had ever shown concern for her safety before, let alone fought for her. She swelled with gratitude for the warrior and, under these dangerous circumstances, she was especially glad that they hadn't parted ways yet.

"I do not see any sign of them!" the man from the north called out.

Lost in thought, it took a moment for Faymia to realize she was being spoken to. "Maybe they think we're dead," she answered.

"It is possible," Dulnear said as he walked back to the fire. "But the Malitae like to keep souvenirs from their fallen opponents. They may be searching for our bodies."

The thought of the strange fighting men from the southern islands looking for her drowned corpse sent shivers down the woman's spine. She leaned closer toward the fire and rubbed her arms. "Thank you for rescuing me," she said, catching his eyes with hers.

The vigilant warrior sat beside her and said, "You are most welcome." He had a look of concentration as he stared into the fire and continued, "There is a very good chance that this is not over with yet. I want you to be safe, but I do not know how much longer I can protect you."

Dulnear's words were curious to Faymia. Ever since she had joined him, he had spoken about parting ways when they reached the north, but never mentioned why. A feeling of sadness settled in her stomach as she pondered what the man was not saying. "I understand," she replied, though she really didn't.

The woman looked down at her feet. They were cold, but feeling had returned, as well as the awareness that her socks were soaking wet. She removed them, grabbed a nearby stick, and used it to dangle them over the fire. As she was drying them, she looked around and noticed a circle of blood growing on the side of Dulnear's shirt. "Your side!" she exclaimed.

The man looked down and recalled, "The Malitae's knife. Fortunately, my coat absorbed most of the blade." Then he lifted his shirt to examine the wound. It was a deep, clean cut that expelled a small but steady trickle of blood.

"What can I do to help?" she offered.

"It is nothing," Dulnear bravely stated as he gently attempted to push the laceration closed.

"It's not nothing," Faymia insisted. "It's still bleeding!"

"Okay," the man conceded with a half-smile. "Take my knife. The tree on which your cloak is hanging has a large scar on the north side of the trunk. Collect some resin with the knife and bring it here."

The woman set her socks down, took the knife, and briskly walked over to the tree, being mindful not to hurt her cold, bare feet. She followed the man's instructions and carefully cut off a large piece of the hard, golden resin from the tree trunk, and returned promptly. When she gave the knife back to Dulnear, he warmed it, with the sap, over the fire. He then smeared the softened, sticky substance over his wound. He also spread some over the cuts on his arms and shoulders. Faymia was impressed that the man hardly seemed fazed by things that would have had other men reeling in pain.

The northerner raised his elbow up and down to make sure that the cut on his side did not reopen. "There, good as new," he assured her with a smile.

The two sat quietly for a while as Faymia resumed hanging her socks over the fire. Eventually, the man from the north stood up and walked over to the cloak and tunic that were hanging from the nearby tree. "They are almost dry," he said. "We need to put out the fire and move off of the bank as soon as possible."

"Where will we go?" Faymia asked.

"Into the woods," he answered. "The longer we stay here, the more we risk the Malitae seeing us from the other side."

"And then?" the woman probed as she put the warm, dry socks back on her feet.

"It is a three-day journey through the forest. After that, we reach farmland and open fields." Dulnear paused and took a deep breath. "I will take you to my estate in Tuas-arum. There I can give you what you need, and then we will have to say goodbye."

Faymia didn't know what he meant by that. She didn't know what the man intended to give her. She only knew that she could trust the kindness in his eyes when he said it. "Okay," she answered, putting on her boots.

The man from the north handed her the dry outer garments. As she put them on, she watched him smooth over their tracks, put out the fire, and toss the burned logs into the river. "This forest can be quite dangerous," he warned. "We have to stay vigilant."

"I'll do my best," she said with concerned eyes. The uneasy feeling she had earlier was beginning to return, but she was determined to stay the course with Dulnear.

"I do not mean to frighten you," her companion continued. "It is only that the wildlife here can be quite aggressive. There is also a chance we have southern warriors following us, and, if we run into other northern folk, they may attack first and ask questions later."

Faymia swallowed. The anxious feeling intensified as she weighed the man's warning. "I will keep both eyes open," she promised, and the two of them walked away from the riverbank and into the woods together.

CHAPTER SEVEN

HOWLS IN THE NIGHT

THE TWO TRAVELERS WALKED THROUGH the woods for several hours. It was challenging, since there were no trails to walk upon and the forest was dense. Late in the afternoon, they found a clearing just big enough to make a small fire and camp for the evening. Faymia was glad to be able to take off her still-damp boots and place them by the fire.

"Would you like something to eat?" Dulnear asked her as she warmed her feet.

"That sounds grand," she answered.

"I'll fetch us something," he said. He then withdrew his knife and disappeared beyond the clearing.

While she waited, the woman thought about the events of the past few days. She knew she had made many bad decisions in her life, and prayed that running away from Tcharron wasn't another one. She only knew that the freedom she now experienced, even though it was mixed with peril and uncertainty, was better than being a slave. She felt a sense of dignity and she wanted to hold onto that. If she were to die running, at least it was because of her choice to run, and not because of the cruel whim of a slaver.

It was almost dark when Dulnear returned with a freshly killed rabbit. As he skinned the animal and prepared it for roasting over the fire, Faymia wondered how many rabbit furs it would take to make him a new coat. Then she smiled to herself in amusement at the thought of the muscular warrior wearing a patchwork rabbit skin coat.

When the animal was done roasting, the man tore it in two and handed half of it to Faymia. "This should warm you up," he said, already biting into his half.

She gratefully accepted the cooked game, hiding that it was uncomfortably hot in her hands. "Thank you," she replied with a hint of a smile.

"I am sorry, I should have let it cool a bit first," Dulnear apologized.

Faymia was surprised. She never mentioned that the meat was too hot and felt she'd hid her reaction well. "I... um..." she muttered.

"I know your looks," the man from the north responded. "That is the face you make when you are trying to hide pain."

The runaway woman was deeply touched by Dulnear's simple statement. She was looking in his direction, but her thoughts drew her focus inward. *He noticed*, she thought to herself. She had never been noticed in such a manner before. She felt seen, and important. The man from the north made her feel like she mattered. Around him, she found it easier to believe that she was good for more than pleasuring men and being the object of crude jokes. "Thank you for noticing," she said. "It's cooling off a bit, and I'm too hungry to put it down anyway." She smiled and bit into the meat, appreciating some cooked food after a long, trying day.

The two sat and enjoyed their rabbit together, staring into the fire and occasionally making small talk. When the woman was done eating, she set the remains of her dinner beside her and slipped on her warm, dry boots. Despite the day, she was content.

After some time, Faymia swallowed and asked, "Dulnear, do you have a woman?" She immediately regretted asking the question, but listened intently for the answer anyway.

Staring into the forest beyond the clearing, the man from the north answered, "I have very high standards."

Something about those words caused the runaway slave to feel discouraged. Only moments earlier she'd felt important, but now the feelings of worthlessness were returning. She began to ask, "What if—"

"Shhhhh!" Dulnear cut her off, still staring into the woods. He then grabbed her leftover rabbit carcass and flung it into the dark forest. The two sat motionless in silence until the sound of wolves fighting over the picked-over rabbit erupted just beyond the clearing.

Immediately, the northern warrior jumped to his feet and began tossing handfuls of twigs and grass into the fire. As he did, the sound of howling could be heard from all directions. Faymia froze with fear. Her eyes were wide, and her heart felt like it was trying to escape from her chest.

"We have to get you off the ground!" the large man exclaimed, and he picked her up as if she was a child. He sprinted to the nearest tall tree and hefted her into it. He then drew his knife and ran off into the darkness.

The sound of howling wolves could be heard from all around. Amidst the grip of crippling panic, Faymia became aware of another sensation. Her hands were throbbing with pain and she could feel blood running down her arms, making its way under the sleeves of her shirt. *What's happening to me?* she wondered. Then it dawned on her; *I'm clinging to a black pine!*

With no sign of Dulnear, pain radiating through her hands and arms, and surrounded by beasts in the darkness, all she could do was whisper prayers into the night.

Dulnear focused on keeping his breath quiet and controlled. He knew that the wolves' hearing was astounding, and they had the advantage in the pitch-black night. He walked slowly and silently through the dark woods, listening for any sound that would indicate the location of the animals. All he could hear was the crackling of the waning fire and his own heartbeat. With his right hand he held his knife out in front of him, ready to plunge it into any beast that came near. The man knew that, in order to survive the night, he had to become the predator and the wolves had to become the prey; but that was far easier said than done. Hoping that the pine sap smeared on his side, arms, and shoulders was masking his scent some, he continued moving, listening, and trying to detect the odor of the deadly animals.

From his right side, the northerner heard the subtle sound of a creature sniffing. He thrust his knife into the darkness, but only made contact with the air. Immediately, he felt teeth sinking into his forearm and pain coursing up to his shoulder like heated lightning. He stifled a yelp, dropped his knife into his left hand, and repeatedly stabbed the wolf in the side of its neck until it released him and fell limp. Ignoring the pain in his arm, he moved quickly in the darkness to remove part of the animal's skin. Cutting off an additional strip of fur, he tied the pelt around his left arm. He reckoned that the pelt would make him smell more like a wolf, and that he could use it to protect himself from another attack.

The man from the north decided to hunt closer to the perimeter of his camp. That way, he would have better visibility from the glow of the campfire. As he made his way, he could see the silhouette of a wolf standing just outside of the clearing. Its eyes were locked onto Faymia as she stood restlessly in the black pine. Dulnear stood silently and waited for the right moment. Then the animal let loose a chilling howl, long and loud. As it did, the warrior dashed toward it and opened its neck with his knife. The wolf whimpered and took its last breath as it dropped to the ground.

From where he stood, Dulnear could see his friend clinging to the tree he'd placed her in. Something wasn't right; she seemed to be struggling to hold on. He began to sprint over to her and felt something chomping at his left leg and right shoulder. Searing pain latched onto him as two wolves tore at his flesh. He could hear their snarls mixed with Faymia's screams from across the clearing.

The man from the north moved his knife to his left hand again and began stabbing at the wolf that was gripping his right shoulder with its fangs. The stabbing seemed to be doing little to slow the beast down as it forcefully whipped its head back and forth with a jaw full of Dulnear's muscle and skin. The man reached down and grabbed the wolf that was attacking his leg and swung it violently into a nearby tree. He could hear its bones cracking, then he tossed the body into the darkness. Just as he was about to grab the wolf latched onto his shoulder, another sprang from the darkness and leapt toward his neck.

Just in time, Dulnear raised his left arm, and the pelt fastened around his arm absorbed some of the bite. No longer able to stab at the wolf on his shoulder, he attempted to shake both animals off with quick, jerking motions. In his furious dance to be free, the man fell backwards onto his back. The fall temporarily stunned the wolf on his shoulder, but it wasn't long before it was on top of him, joining the other animal that was trying to tear at his neck. Desperation overcame the man from the north and he stabbed wildly at the beasts with his right hand while trying to beat them back with his left. Though he was able to injure the wolf nearest the knife-wielding hand, it didn't seem to do much to slow the carnivore down. He knew that if he stopped fighting even for a second, he would be dead, and his friend would not be far behind.

Just then, a shriek could be heard from across the clearing, drawing the beasts' attention. The wounded northerner looked up to see that the woman had fallen out of the tree and now the wolves were running toward her as she scrambled to her feet.

Faymia quickly reached for a branch that was lying partially out of the fire and began swinging the fiery end at the wolves, stopping them in their tracks. As they bared their fangs and barked ferociously, Dulnear approached from behind and plunged his knife into the side of one of them. His exhausted, bloodied arms were heavy and weak, but he willed them to cut the life out of the animal. With the surviving wolf's attention now on the large man, Faymia smashed at its skull with her burning branch, stunning it, thus bringing its attention back onto her.

The man from the north crawled behind the monster and tore open its neck with his blade. As blood flowed from the beast, he watched it die with a mixture of satisfaction and sadness.

The warrior stood to make sure his friend was all right. As he approached her, a strange sensation overcame him. The woods spun, and all went dark. He fainted, falling back to the ground.

It was dark, and the sights and sounds that swirled around Dulnear seemed distorted and difficult to discern, much like what one experiences when suddenly pulled underwater. The man concentrated hard to focus on where he was and what was happening. Eventually, he found himself standing in blackness, able to block out the chaos around him, but still disoriented.

A muffled voice called out to him from the darkness. As the voice became clearer and closer, the man from the north could hear it calling, "Marhail! Marhail!" It caused the hair on his arms to stand on end and sent a chill down his spine.

Dulnear was familiar with the word, for he had yelled it many times before rushing to battle with an enemy. It was intended to instill fear in an opponent, as it was a call to rain death down upon them. In the past, he would simply brush the word off; but this time was different, for he was truly afraid. His hands shook, and he desperately looked around to find the source of the haunting wail. But deep and cold it continued to sound from the darkness.

Suddenly, the blurred shapes and colors all around him came into focus and the fallen Tromdel stood before him. His skin was pale, his hair and beard matted with blood, and maggots clung to the fatal wound in his chest. "Marhail!" he repeated with a sinister grin. "Soon, son of Athnear, you will suffer a fate worse than mine!"

"I am only dreaming," Dulnear retorted apprehensively. "My life is in the hands of the Great Father."

"Do you really think sacrificing yourself for those children will make up for all of the blood you've spilled?" the ghost asked with a laugh that dripped black with malice. He then drew his sword and raised it over his head to strike.

Dulnear reached for his weapon but it was not there. Panicking, he answered, "I do not—" but he was interrupted when two northerners appeared behind him. Violently, they jerked him to the ground and held him there, while a third appeared over him with a long, rusty knife. The third northerner plunged the knife into Dulnear's chest and carved a crude hole. He then reached in and took out the warrior's still-beating heart.

The dreaming Dulnear watched as his heart was held aloft. He tried to pray for help, but no words would sound from his mouth. Then he tried reaching for the heart so he could put it back inside his chest, but his arms were too weak to fight his attackers. Hopelessness and fear encompassed him like a burning blanket wrapped around his body, and he believed that true death was only a breath away.

In an instant, Dulnear was alone, lying on the ground. All was black except for a trace of light that shined down on him. He lifted his head to survey the hole in his chest. The hopelessness and fear gave way as an all-consuming feeling of emptiness grew within him and the world faded to darkness.

"Marhail," he heard the familiar voice whisper again from the black.

"It is just a dream," the man from the north whispered to himself. "It is just a dream."

The next morning, Dulnear woke to pain all over his body. He was partially covered by Faymia's cloak and had fresh layers of pine resin smeared across his wounds. The larger lacerations were wrapped in small strips cut from the bottom of the cloak. The woman was tending the fire and didn't notice he was awake yet. "Faymia," he called out to her with a weak voice. "What happened?"

She rushed to his side and answered, "You fell unconscious; I couldn't wake you."

"Did we get all of the wolves?" the man asked.

"I believe we did," she answered. "There was no more

howling after you passed out. I dragged their bodies past the southern edge of the clearing. They have a terrible odor!"

"That they do," Dulnear agreed. "I am glad you are safe."

The runaway slave smiled with her eyes. "And I'm glad you're awake. You gave me quite a scare."

The hard traveling, lack of sleep, and injuries were taking their toll on the mighty northerner, and he knew it. He tried to look strong for his friend. "I am sorry. I really am fine," he assured her.

Faymia spoke softly, "I know your looks. That's the face you make when you're trying to hide pain."

The man from the north gave a tired smile and examined the sap-covered wounds on his arm and shoulder. He was grateful that his friend tended to them in the night, but they still throbbed with pain. "I suppose it would be beneficial to rest a little while longer," he admitted.

"That's a good idea," she said. "I'll see if I can gather some berries for us."

Dulnear coughed and laid his head down. "Do not go too far from the clearing," he instructed. He then closed his eyes and drifted back into a restless sleep.

A little while later, the man opened his eyes again to find his friend sitting nearby nibbling on berries and poking at the fire. "How long did I sleep?" he asked groggily as he raised his head.

Faymia moved to sit next to him and placed her hand on his shoulder. "It's mid-afternoon," she said.

"I'm sorry for sleeping so long," Dulnear apologized. "I should catch us some dinner." As he attempted to sit up, pain coursed through his shoulder, taking his breath away. He winced and laid his head back down.

"It's okay," Faymia answered. "I've already taken care of that," and she pointed toward a dead squirrel nearby.

The man from the north reached out for the woman's hand, exhaled, and said, "Thank you. Your kindness means very much to me."

"You're very welcome," she said. Then she paused, and her expression changed as she asked, "Dulnear, what is a Marhail?"

The feelings that accompanied the previous night's dream washed over the injured warrior. He remembered the blackness, Tromdel's voice, and watching his heart being cut out and held out of reach. He released the woman's hand, swallowed, and said hesitantly, "It is a curse intended to strike fear into an enemy."

The woman made a pained expression. "You were saying it in your sleep last night," she explained.

"I am very sorry," the man said. "I did not mean to frighten you."

Faymia looked at Dulnear's face for a moment. Her head tilted sideways and her voice softened. "Why do we have to part ways when we reach Tuas-arum?" she asked.

For a moment, Dulnear wrestled with whether or not he should tell Faymia what he was doing, but he had grown fond of her and felt that he could trust her with his story. He told her about leaving Tuas-arum to escape the violent ways of his people. He told her about his friends, Son and Maren, and their small farm in Laor. He also told her about killing Tromdel after he followed him south and challenged him to a death duel. "I am going to offer myself in restitution to Tromdel's family," he explained.

The woman had a look of disbelief. She asked indignantly, "What do you have to make restitution for? If anything, his family should be apologizing that their blowhard kin tried to kill you!"

"I know," the man from the north said. "But northerners do not live by the same sense of fairness and justice that others do. It is a destructive code of existence. From an early age, we are taught that physical dominance over others is what brings the highest esteem. We are raised on violence, hatred, and revenge. It is our way of life." He then looked away, his eyes beginning to fill with tears. "Son and Maren will never be truly safe if I do not do this. I love them, and this is the only way."

Faymia's eyes began to turn red and she wiped her nose with the handkerchief Dulnear had given her earlier. "What will happen when you offer yourself in restitution?" she asked.

"That depends," he answered. "My life will be in the hands of Tromdel's family. I will plead for their forgiveness, but…" then he hesitated. "It is most likely that they will execute me."

"No!" the woman said with voice raised. "You cannot do this! There has to be another way!"

"I wish that there was," said Dulnear. "Vengeance will be their only priority. They will come for me, and they will use the children to make me suffer. This is the only way."

Faymia cried. Her shoulders shook and she reached out to hold Dulnear's hand once again. "But you could fight them, you could defend the children."

"That is true," the man admitted. "But that will only beget more violence. This way, the circle is broken."

"It's not fair!" the woman exclaimed. "It shouldn't be this way." She sat silent for a moment. Her tears subsided, and she looked as if all of the strength was drained from her body.

Dulnear continued, gently squeezing her hand, "Sometimes the wisest thing to do is the most difficult thing, especially when it is for those you love. I did not want to leave the children, and now I do not want to leave you. But I cannot allow myself to be tempted by self-preservation if I want to do the right thing."

"I won't leave you," she said as she quietly began to weep again.

"If you do not, then you will watch me die," the warrior said as a tear fell from his eye.

"Then I will hold your hand as you pass into the next life!" Faymia exclaimed, then she laid her head down on her friend's chest and cried some more.

Dulnear wrapped his arm around the woman's shoulder and the two of them wept together until they ran out of tears and just laid there quietly. Eventually, Faymia asked, "It's getting late. Would you like me to cook the squirrel?"

"No," the man answered. "I am just fine as I am."

The woman stayed where she was and closed her red, swollen eyes.

Soon, the day faded completely and they both fell asleep. It was a sound sleep, the best the man from the north had enjoyed since leaving Laor.

CHAPTER EIGHT
HOME NO MORE

D AYS LATER, DULNEAR AND FAYMIA made their way out of the gradually fading woods that opened up to lush, rolling country. The gray, cool, late afternoon sky stretched over fields of grass and grain, and large homes and barns could be seen in the far distance.

As they stood and gazed out over the new landscape, the woman whispered, "It's beautiful here."

"This is Tuas-arum," the warrior said with sentimentality in his voice. "And why are you whispering?"

"I don't know," she admitted. "I've just never seen a view so peaceful-looking." She paused, then added, "I guess I was just expecting something else."

"Did you think men would be running about, chasing each other with torches and swords?" he asked in jest.

Faymia gave an embarrassed smile and said, "Maybe a little."

"The beauty of this place is what made it so difficult for me to leave," the man from the north explained. "You cannot see them yet, but beyond these rolling hills are the Petraig Mountains, the most majestic mountains in Aun.

I have spent much time climbing and exploring them. It is where I learned to forage, and camp."

The runaway slave looked over the landscape with a puzzled expression, then asked, "Are there no roads?"

Amused by her question, Dulnear explained, "Yes, we have roads, and cities, too. However, we are staying far from them. If I were to be seen, word that I am here would travel to Tromdel's family faster than I would like it to, and I would very much like to visit my estate first."

"I understand," the woman said. "At least we're not traveling through the forest anymore."

"Yes, but we will need to stay within the edges of it tonight. I would not want anyone to see our campfire. If the owner of this land found us, he would likely assume we are members of a rival clan and assault us before we had a chance to explain why we are here," he said.

As the two made camp amidst a cluster of trees, Dulnear worked with a nervous energy. Being in his homeland gave him strength, but his purpose for being there filled him with sadness. It was a paradox of feeling that caused him to wish his heart would choose one or the other.

As Faymia used the waning daylight to find berries, the northern warrior stoked the fire and imagined what it was going to be like when he walked on his own land again. He thought about the huge oak tree that he'd persuaded his younger brother to jump from when they were children. He thought about the many hours spent learning from his father; and, when he concentrated hard, he could remember the face of his mother. As he grew older, the memories of her became harder to hold onto.

Though she died giving birth to his brother, she forever held a special place in his heart.

Faymia appeared next to him with an armful of berries, pulling the man from his memories. They sat together sharing them quietly, looking into the fire. Eventually, the woman broke the silence. "How far is your house from here?" she asked.

"Not far," he answered. "We should be there in two nights." He then pointed to a place on the fading horizon and explained, "We are only a few estates away."

As she wiped her hands on the grass, she looked at her friend and asked, "Do you miss your home?"

Dulnear inhaled deeply, then exhaled. "There is much to miss. But there is also much that I am happy to leave behind. Home, family, childhood friendships; these things shape a young life profoundly. But for me, these were irreparably broken, so I decided to seek out surroundings that call out better things from me."

The woman paused for a moment with an understanding expression, then asked, "Was it difficult to leave?"

"Difficult like setting a badly broken bone is difficult," he explained. "It hurts every day, but I know it was for the best." Then he added, "If you do not set a broken leg properly, then you risk walking crooked for the rest of your life."

"I know what you mean," she said. "My mother was born with a bent foot. She told me that, every day, her father had to twist it in the proper direction. She hated the pain and would protest continually. But, if not for the painful twisting, she never would have been able to walk properly."

The two sat a while longer, finishing their berries and watching the fire until the sky was completely dark. As they sat together, a question began to stir in Dulnear. "Faymia, if you had not become a slave, what would you have done?"

The question seemed to surprise her. She squinted at the fire, thought, and answered, "When I was a young girl, my mother had a friend that would take me hunting with him. I was terrified at first, but he taught me how to track an animal, how to move about without being heard, and how to skin and prepare it for dinner. That is when I caught my first squirrel. The man and my mother were not friends for very long, but I grew to love hunting in the short time that I knew him, and dreamt of doing it for the rest of my life."

"I can definitely see you succeeding as a hunter," the man from the north said with a smile. "You managed to follow me without being heard, and that is not easy."

Faymia looked at her friend and smiled. "Well, thank you for aiming your knife at a tree instead of me," she laughed.

With an awkward expression on his face, Dulnear asked, "Who said I was aiming at the tree?" and gave a chuckle.

"Do you mean you almost killed me?" Faymia replied, looking shocked.

The man from the north smiled and laughed. "I am making a joke," he admitted.

The runaway slave exhaled with relief and shook her head. "You almost had me."

Dulnear looked at Faymia's face for a moment. "I am glad you ran away, and I am glad you followed me."

The woman's smile widened and she moved closer to the warrior. Together, they watched the fire until it was just a flicker in the night.

When Dulnear went to sleep that night, he had dreams of his home. They were not the usual dreams of turmoil or violence but of happy boyhood times and fond memories. They were dreams of peace.

Two days later, the travelers had reached Dulnear's land. It was overgrown and neglected but situated on lush, rolling hills. Clusters of oak trees stood like giants huddled together for protection against the wind, and a hint of the Petraig Mountains could be seen in the distance.

When they stepped onto the grounds, the man from the north stopped, closed his eyes, and breathed in deeply. The smell of the air, the sound of the breeze, and the feel of the earth beneath his feet seemed to carry greater potency than they ever had before as memories of life there rushed to flood his mind.

"Are you okay?" Faymia asked.

"I suppose," he answered. "It was over a season ago that I left here. It feels like longer, and it feels like less time. So much pain and happiness, I don't know which to feel."

The woman hugged his scarred arm and replied, "I

wish there was something I could do to make this easier for you."

The warrior looked at his friend and said with a wistful smile, "You already have."

Faymia returned his smile and asked, "Where is your house?"

"Over the next hill," he answered. "We should be there by dark."

As the two walked slowly through the fields, Dulnear shared the stories of his life on the estate. He showed her where his family hosted parties, where he would like to hide and read as a boy, and the place where his father and brother died defending themselves from a nearby clan. "I do not even know what they were fighting about," he explained. "I had already begun to grow weary of the conflict and wanted to stay out of it. I often wonder how things would be different if I would have chosen to fight alongside them that day." He had more to say about the matter but noticed that the sky was almost dark, so he suggested that they make their way to the house.

They approached it from the south side. The structure was more akin to a castle than a house. It stood three stories high and was made of stone. The roof was steep and covered in slate tiles, and the four corners of the house were guarded by high, pointed turrets. It was clearly built to withstand the onslaught of time and conflict, and had changed little since Dulnear was a boy. As they walked closer, an excitement rose up inside of him. He began to quicken his pace until something caught his eye that stopped him in his tracks.

"Do not move," he whispered to Faymia as he held his arm out.

"What is it?" she quietly asked.

"Over there. Look in the second-floor window," he said.

The woman strained her eyes. "What do you see?"

"Light flickering against the wall of the drawing room," the man answered. "That should not be. Be very quiet, and we will get a little closer."

The two crouched and moved silently toward the house. When they reached the thick, wild garden, the light became more visible, and Dulnear pointed it out to Faymia once more.

"I see it now," she said, squinting. "What are we going to do?"

"We shall enter through the back," the man from the north said. "I will find out who this intruder is."

The two made their way to the eastern side of the house, which held the back entrance and an entrance to the kitchen. The large warrior went to go in through the back entrance and discovered that the lock had already been pried open. His nostrils flared, and anger began to grow at the thought of someone violating his home.

He ducked inside the house, with the woman close behind. The door opened to a narrow hallway, and on their left was another door that served as the entrance to a small room. It was pitch-black in the house, but the man from the north moved through it as though it were broad daylight.

On the far side of the room was a window, and under it was a small table holding a lantern and a tinderbox loaded with brimstone matches. Dulnear walked across to the window, felt for the matches, and lit the lantern, revealing a dusty library that looked as if it had not been touched for several seasons.

There was a large desk toward the east side of the room, and four padded leather chairs situated in the middle. There were well-stocked bookshelves covering the surface of all four walls, reaching almost to the ceiling. Resting on the tops of the bookshelves were what seemed to be trophies.

Faymia strained her eyes as she gazed at the objects lining the top of the shelves, then gasped, "Those look like hands!"

"They are hands," the warrior replied with a measure of shame in his voice. "Here, it is customary to display the right hand of your fallen opponent, like a prize. It is a rather crude form of boasting. I am sorry that you had to see it."

The woman looked across the tops of all of the bookshelves with eyes wide and mouth agape. "How many are there?" she asked.

The man from the north lowered his eyes and answered, "I do not know. Please do not judge me too harshly, though I will not blame you if you do. It is because of these sorts of things that I fled the north."

Faymia swallowed and turned her eyes toward her friend. "It's okay. I'm just not used to seeing such things. I know this isn't you anymore."

"Thank you," the man said with a sigh. "There are many more throughout the house. Please do not be alarmed by them." He continued, "Up the stairs is my father's room. I will need to retrieve a few things from there before we confront this intruder. Be as quiet as you can."

The woman nodded, and the two of them left the library and proceeded further down the narrow hallway. At the end of it was another door. Dulnear opened it slowly, keeping a keen eye out for unwelcome visitors. The door opened up to an expansive, wood-paneled foyer. To their right was a grand staircase, and beyond that was a dining room containing an enormous table and a wide stone fireplace.

The man from the north held out the lantern. Its light danced against the high ceiling, and large paintings and tapestries could be seen along the walls. They made their way to the staircase and slowly climbed it to the second floor. Each creak from the stairs caused his heart to race a little faster.

When they reached the second floor, the staircase opened up to a broad hallway before turning and continuing its ascent to the third floor. Dulnear dimmed the flame on his lantern and pointed to a door in front of them. They stealthily went through it and closed it behind themselves.

"This was my father's chamber," the man whispered. He raised the flame on his lantern again and looked around. It was a large room with an equal amount of paintings and weapons adorning the walls. There was a canopy bed in the center of the room and a wide wardrobe along the same wall as the entrance. The room looked mostly undisturbed, but the bed appeared to have been slept in.

Quietly, Dulnear opened the wardrobe and took out a long fur coat and a bag, much like the ones he had lost in the river. He smelled the coat, and memories of his father came over him as if they had happened earlier that day. He put it on and reached back into the wardrobe. He inhaled deeply and withdrew a sword that looked similar to the one he had lost. He examined the weapon, remembering his father's fondness for the craftsmanship of the blade and the heft of the hilt. Noticing that his companion was watching with raised eyebrows and a focused gaze, he explained, "This is Renaire, my father's sword. I placed it here when he died, and it hasn't been touched since."

"It is a fine sword," she offered with an expression that said she wasn't sure what to say.

"It has always been my favorite, besides my own," the man from the north said as he strapped it around his waist, then covered it with the coat. He also took a couple of smaller swords off of the adjacent wall and concealed them as well. Then he surveyed the wall a bit further and took down a fierce-looking sword and smiled. "This one suits you," he said as he handed it to his friend. "My mother and father had always hoped to give me a sister, and this was going to be hers."

"I can't," Faymia responded. "It wouldn't be right to take it."

"I am the last of my family, and soon all of this will be abandoned," Dulnear explained. "It would comfort me to know that a friend such as you had this."

"Thank you," she accepted humbly. As she strained to examine the weapon under the lantern light, she observed, "Your women must be large, much like the men."

It dawned on Dulnear that the sword was too large for Faymia. "I am sorry," he said. "Yes, our women are taller than southern women." He then took a smaller sword from the wall and handed it to her. "This one looks just right."

Faymia looked over the new sword and smiled, thanking the man. As she belted the sword around her waist, the northern warrior reached higher up the wall and took down a beautifully ornate wooden bow and a quiver stocked with arrows. "And no hunter would be properly equipped without a bow," he said as he handed it to her.

Faymia's eyes grew big as she took it and ran her fingers over the bow's carvings. "I don't know what to say," she said gratefully.

"Just say that you will use it," he said. It made the man feel good to show generosity, even in the midst of a trying situation.

"I will," she said as she slung the quiver and bow over her shoulder. Just then, she noticed that Dulnear had an amused grin smeared across his face. "What's so funny?" she asked.

"It is just that those child's weapons are the perfect size for you," he said.

Faymia chuckled in a low voice, "Well, we can't all be overgrown hay burners," she retorted playfully.

"Excuse me," the man said. "I may look like a horse, but, most days, I smell much better."

Faymia covered her mouth to silence another giggle, and Dulnear enjoyed watching her try to hold it back. Just then, the sound of glass breaking could be heard from the drawing room down the hall.

They both froze for a moment, then the man from

the north instinctively reached for the handle of Renaire while placing himself between the woman and the door. In the silence, he waited for the sound of footsteps to come, but none came.

"I am going to look in the drawing room," he told his friend softly. "You wait here."

Faymia reached out and squeezed the man's arm. "I want to come too," she said in a brave whisper.

"No. Please wait here," he instructed, before handing off the lantern to her and reentering the hall.

Dulnear withdrew his father's sword and held it ready as he made his way toward the flickering light that was coming from the drawing room. His palms became sweaty and he took a deep breath. He didn't know who he was going to find, but he was determined to make them understand the lack of wisdom associated with forcing an entry into his house.

The warrior silently opened the drawing room door. He was moved by many more memories, and had to remind himself to remain focused. The room was lit by an oil lamp and a few mostly burned candles that flickered against the high walls. There were also glowing embers in the fireplace from a fire that had gone out earlier. There were large portraits covering the walls, several of which had been ruined by gashes across their faces. There were also bottles strewn about and an absurd amount of dirty dishes. The wall opposite the door held a large window that was bordered by a stuffed sofa and chair. Sleeping on the furniture were Thorndel and Brunnlyn, Tromdel's brother and cousin.

CHAPTER NINE
A FUTILE GESTURE

'T IS AN ANSWER TO MY *dilemma*, Dulnear thought to himself. *Those who would seek to harm me are asleep before me. I need only to slay them in their slumber and never return.*

It was a dark chain of thoughts, but the man from the north tried to assuage his conscience by thinking of his young friends in Laor, and how they needed him. He was also considering Faymia and her fate once he was gone. Besides, these good-for-nothings broke into his home and disgraced the memories of his family. What he was about to do, they had coming. He tightened his grip on the hilt of his sword, stood over Thorndel, and raised the blade over his head. The brutish, drunken vengeance seeker was oblivious to the death that laid suspended a mere handbreadth above his chest.

As the warrior stood there, envisioning his kill, he noticed a light growing in the corner of his eye. He glanced toward the door and saw Faymia standing pale and silent, with eyes wide in disbelief.

A feeling of shame descended upon the man. He sheathed his sword and briefly lowered his head. Then he quietly walked over to his friend and looked past her as he thought about what to say. Finally, he met eyes with her and whispered, "These are the men that are seeking revenge for Tromdel's death."

"I understand," the woman replied. Her eyes were pink and her hands were shaking. "But it isn't right to kill them in their sleep."

Just then, Dulnear remembered a lesson that his father had given him many times. *The right thing is often the hard thing. There is no honor in taking the easy path.* In that moment, he wanted more than anything for that to be untrue. He yearned for this to be the exception but he knew that it was not. "I am sorry," he said, cooling his aggression. "You are right."

"Dulnear," Faymia said, with tears forming and lip quivering.

"Yes?" he whispered.

After a pause to maintain her composure, she continued, "I want you to live. More than anything, I want to leave here with you. But you would never know peace if you deviated from what you came to do."

A tear now ran down the man's cheek as he contemplated his friend's words. He thought about the journey south, the time spent with the boy Son and the girl Maren, his newfound friendship with Faymia, and seeing his home violated by Thorndel and Brunnlyn. It had all led to this moment. All he wanted was to be a peaceful man, and now the price of that peace brought a crushing weight upon his heart. "Thank you," he said, and the two embraced.

There was much crying, though it was done silently.

Dulnear's arms lifted Faymia off of the floor as she wept into the fur shoulder of his long coat. When their tears had subsided, he set her down and looked at her face for a moment. "Stay behind me," he said. "There is little chance that they would want to harm you, but I prefer not to take any chances."

The woman nodded in acknowledgement and stepped away from the man so that she stood just outside the drawing room's doorway. The heavy-hearted warrior then slowly turned toward the sleeping northerners. "Kerraic," he said calmly and clearly from across the room. It was a casual northern greeting that was usually given in public when one wanted to be polite but didn't particularly desire conversation. There was no stirring, and no reply. "Kerraic!" he said again, with a growl in his voice.

This time, the resentful intruders groggily sprang to their feet with swords drawn. Squinting through the sleep in his eyes and shaking the booze-laden haze from his thoughts, Thorndel swept the curly black hair from his bearded face and grunted, "I cannot believe it. It is the mighty Dulnear! We were going to come track you down but you came to us instead. How very convenient."

After months of imagining how their confrontation would play out, the man from the north realized that none of it was going the way he thought it would. He had hoped to help his friend, enjoy his home for his last few days, and surrender himself to Tromdel's father to make restitution. "What are you doing in my house?" he asked with a chill in his voice.

Thorndel answered, "You took my brother, so I found it fitting that I should take your home. Why would you be so foolish as to return here?" He then peeked behind the warrior and asked with wrinkled forehead, "And who is that ragamuffin of a woman you brought with you?"

Anger was beginning to stir in Dulnear's chest. He could feel it tighten and tried to remain composed. *Stay the course*, he reminded himself. *Go deep into the difficult thing.* "I am here to make restitution," he declared, ignoring the question.

"Restitution?!" Thorndel questioned indignantly. He then laughed sarcastically and said, "You probably came to slay me the way you did my brother!"

Dulnear took a deep breath. "I merely defended myself against Tromdel," he said. "It is he who stole my Credreact and challenged me to a death duel." The penitent warrior noticed that Brunnlyn had lowered his sword and was listening intently. He turned his attention toward him now and continued, "I begged him to stay his sword, but he insisted on fighting until one of us was dead."

Brunnlyn swallowed. His blue eyes were sympathetic, and he looked as if he was about to say something when Thorndel interrupted, "I care not why you did it! All that matters is that his blood is on your hands, and now my only desire is for you to join him."

The anger inside of Dulnear continued to grow. Frustrated by Thorndel's unreasonable desire for revenge, he placed his hand on the hilt of his sword and retorted, "He was a bloodthirsty braggart with a death wish!"

Thorndel took a step toward Dulnear, shouting, "I will give you braggart! I will finish what my brother started!"

"Only if you wish to die too!" he replied, partly unsheathing his sword. Just then, the warrior felt a gentle hand on his back as his friend tried to calm him. She said nothing, but he knew by her touch that she was reminding him to exercise restraint and calmly do what he came to do. He removed his hand from his weapon, held it up, and said, "Wait! I truly did come to make restitution. Please take me to your father. He may do with me as he pleases." He held his hostility back, hoping it would defuse the other's combativeness.

"Why should I trust you?" Thorndel barked. "You probably want to kill him as well!"

Dulnear said nothing as he turned his back toward his accusers and knelt with hands out and eyes closed. It was a position northerners would assume when they accidentally injured a training partner and they were giving them the opportunity to injure them in return. As he waited for the other northerners' response, the room seemed to sway like a boat at sea, and there was a dreamlike quality to the moment.

Thorndel growled, raised his sword and lunged toward the kneeling northerner, but before he could strike, Brunnlyn shouted, "Stop!"

Thorndel shot a steely gaze at his cousin. "Why? This is the opportunity we've been waiting for!"

"There is no honor in striking him down like this. There would be no glorious tale of battle," he answered. He then put his sword away and continued, "Besides, I believe he speaks the truth. We should take him to your father."

The raging Thorndel lowered his sword and paused. "Very well," he said, and he struck Dulnear above the ear with his fist, causing him to totter as he knelt. "We shall take him to Father right now."

Thorndel and Brunnlyn took Dulnear back to one of the estate's outbuildings as Faymia followed silently, fighting back tears. They attached a yoke to his neck and shoulders and hitched him to a cart. "It is a long walk to my estate," Thorndel said. "You shall pull us so that we have the energy to execute you, should my father give the order." He then laughed as he looked at Brunnlyn for approval.

Dulnear said nothing as the two fur-clad northerners climbed into the seat of the cart, greatly increasing the weight on his shoulders. He pulled the cart out of the outbuilding, each step feeling like the labor of a thousand. As he made his way around the house and toward the road, he peered through the darkness to try and capture one last glance of his home. Unfortunately, the torches that Brunnlyn had attached to the sides of the cart gave off only enough light to see a very short distance.

As Dulnear approached the road that curved around the northern edge of his estate, he stumbled, causing the yoke's bow to choke him. When he coughed, Faymia ran to his side. "Stay away from him if you want to keep your head!" Thorndel erupted as he caught her shoulder with the tip of an ox whip.

Startled, the woman yelped and reached back to rub her shoulder.

"It is okay," Dulnear whispered to his friend, then muscled the cart onto the road. Once there, the load was easier to pull, but nonetheless an immense strain. The woman fell back behind them, whispering prayers and wiping her eyes.

Thorndel glanced at Faymia, then back to Dulnear. "So tell me, Harbem, who is this southern woman who cares so much for a cold-blooded killer like yourself?" he asked through a pretentious grin.

The yoked warrior didn't appreciate being called Harbem, for it was a derogatory term that meant dead man. He knew that it was true though, since Thorndel would likely persuade his father to remove his head from his shoulders. Even so, he remained silent and did not answer the question.

"Speak!" the vindictive northerner demanded as he stung the side of Dulnear's head with the whip.

Dulnear's face turned red and his nostrils flared. The anger in his chest was returning. "What is it to you?" he asked defiantly.

"Speak, or I shall hitch her to this cart for the return journey!" Thorndel shouted with another crack of the whip.

"She is just a friend. We met in Ahmcathare," he answered as the pain from being struck by fist and whip pulsated with increasing intensity.

"Just a friend?!" the obnoxious brute retorted. "She does not look like the type of person you would waste your time with. She is probably a prostitute!"

"No!" Dulnear denied. "She is just a barmaid. We happened to be traveling in the same direction and became friends."

"I do not believe you!" Thorndel insisted. "Perhaps if she sat up here with us, your memory would improve. Bring her here!" he barked at his cousin.

The blonde-haired, full-bearded Brunnlyn jumped down off of the wagon and was upon Faymia before she could escape. He took her arm and began pulling her toward the cart as she struggled to release herself.

"No!" Dulnear yelled as he stopped pulling the cart. "She is of no consequence!" The northerner felt his anger turn into rage. He was helpless to do anything to aid his friend, and wished he was free to wield his sword to defend her.

Brunnlyn hesitated for a moment. He looked over his shoulder toward Dulnear, and then back toward Faymia. Without a word, he scooped her up with his right arm and carried her back to the cart as she flailed even harder to be free. When he got back into the seat, he placed her on his right side and whispered something to her.

When Dulnear noticed that his friend was sitting to Brunnlyn's right, rather than in between the two louts, he relaxed a bit and began to pull the cart again.

"Now, tell me the truth," Thorndel continued. "Who is she?"

"I have already told you she is a barmaid that I met while traveling past Ahmcathare. She said she had always wanted to visit the north, so I offered to be her guide. If you are so interested in her, then you may ask her for a date!" Dulnear replied, keeping it hidden that Faymia was a runaway slave.

"You are not amusing!" Thorndel huffed as he cracked the whip again. He cackled and added, "You are the worst guide ever! You brought her here to watch you die, and now she has to find her own way home." He then turned his attention to the woman, and continued, "Perhaps you would like to stay with me. I might find you useful as a house slave!"

Faymia shrieked, leapt from the cart, and began running in the direction from which they came. As she did, Dulnear stopped the cart and listened to her flee into the darkness. The tightness in his chest subsided as her footsteps became more faint in the distance.

"Go get her!" the dark-haired ruffian commanded his cousin.

Without moving, Brunnlyn replied, "Leave her be. We are here to avenge your brother, not waste our time on vagabond travelers."

"Hrmff," Thorndel seethed. "I suppose you are right. Besides, I need to focus my thoughts on how I will make this murderer's death as painful as possible."

Dulnear was relieved that his friend was out of the cart and free of the two goons. He hoped that she would go back to his house and take whatever valuables she could carry. He hoped that she would make her way someplace far away and safe, maybe even to Laor, where Son and Maren were. As he continued closer to Thorndel's father's estate, a sense of urgency to get the ordeal over with came over him. His pace quickened and his resolve grew as he pulled his accusers into the night.

CHAPTER TEN
DEATH OF A WARRIOR

WHEN THEY ARRIVED AT THE estate of Thorndel and his father, Shenndel, it was late, and dark, and the morning dew was already beginning to form on the ground. It was a smaller property than Dulnear's, with a more modestly sized house. The dwelling was a two-story cottage with a thatched roof and had none of the defensive properties that Dulnear's impressive home possessed.

As they slowly moved over the steep path that led to the house, Thorndel began to yell, "Father! I brought you something! Come see who has returned!" There was no stirring in the lightless house, so the vindictive northerner leapt out of the cart and ran ahead, shouting, "Father, I have returned with Tromdel's murderer! Come out and see!"

When they were all just a stone's throw from the front door, a spark could be seen in one of the second-floor windows, and then a lantern glowing. It disappeared for a moment, and then reappeared on the first floor just before the door swung open. Shenndel stood there. His face displayed fatigue and agitation, and it was surrounded by unruly white hair and an equally unruly white beard. A long fur coat was draped over his nightclothes. "You found him!" he exclaimed, and he walked out to examine the exhausted, yoked Dulnear.

He held out his lantern and looked sternly into the eyes of the man who had ended his son's life.

"I told you I would bring him to you!" Thorndel exclaimed.

"Be quiet!" Shenndel demanded as he continued to gaze at Dulnear. He then inhaled sharply, spit in his face, and slapped him repeatedly. "So, you thought you could hide in the south and rob me of my Doltais. You are not so clever, son of Athnear!" Then he turned his attention back toward Thorndel. "Well done, my son. Where did you find him?"

Thorndel answered with a series of mutters that were barely discernible. His expression went from one of total victory to one of veiled embarrassment. Finally, Dulnear broke in, "He found me at my estate."

"What?!" Shenndel bellowed with indignation. "But you left to search for him several days ago!"

"He only arrived yesterday," his son explained, still looking embarrassed.

The old man's eyes tightened and his lip curled. "So you have been at his estate this whole time?!" he asked.

"Well, yes, we were destroying his family memories," Thorndel gloated. "You should see the paintings in the drawing room."

"Paintings do not fight back!" his father exploded. "He could have traveled all the way to Saol while you were busy tearing up heirlooms!"

"And drinking my wine," Dulnear added, still hitched to the cart. He found the exchange between the father and son amusing, and didn't mind adding fuel to the fire.

Looking both irritated and inquisitive, Shenndel stared at the yoked man. "Why would you return to your estate? Do you have a death wish?" he asked.

"Sir, I did not have a quarrel with your son Tromdel," Dulnear began. "He tracked me down near Blackcloth and stole my Cre-dreact in order to draw me into a duel. Though I pleaded with him not to fight, he would not relent. I slew him during our battle, and I have come here to make restitution."

"He lies!" Thorndel blurted out. "He would have killed us in our sleep if not for my keen senses."

"It is not true," Dulnear explained. "He and Brunnlyn were asleep in the drawing room when I arrived. My sword was drawn and poised to strike but I stayed my hand and announced my presence to them instead. I am here to make things right, and end the circle of vengeance between us."

"It is he who is lying, Father," Thorndel accused. "He even had a southern woman with him to help carry out his scheme."

Shenndel's eyebrows shot up and the wrinkles on his forehead became more pronounced. "Woman? Where is she now?" he asked in a demanding tone.

"She fled while we were on the road here," his son answered. "Brunnlyn clumsily let her escape."

"Brunnlyn, is this true?" the old man asked, turning his attention to his nephew.

The man paused, then answered, "Uncle, I believe

Dulnear speaks the truth. He could have slain us in our drunken sleep but he did not."

"He COULD not!" Thorndel shouted.

"Enough!" his father scoffed as he struck him across the face with the back of his hand. "Your words are giving me a headache. It is late, and with what remains of this night, I will sleep on what I am going to do." He then addressed Dulnear, "But first, tell me, how many of my kinsmen's hands are displayed on your shelves? Twenty? Thirty?" He then leaned in closer to the warrior and waited with an expression of malice.

The penitent man's stomach felt as if a hole had just been opened in it. His head was hot and his knees weakened. He tried to tally, in his mind, how many hands were arranged throughout his house, and how many of them belonged to members of Shenndel's clan. He lost count, took a deep breath, and finally answered, "I do not know."

"Speak up!" the old man commanded.

"I do not know," Dulnear repeated. "Please forgive me. I no longer wish to make war." He then lowered his head in shame for the sins of his past, and of his family's role in the cycle of northern violence.

Shenndel's face turned crimson and his hands began to shake. He snatched Thorndel's sword and held it over Dulnear's neck. His breath was noisy and he ground his teeth. He then closed his eyes and slowly regained his composure. Once it had returned, he ordered his son and nephew, "Leave him hitched to the cart till morning, and watch him." He then handed the sword back to Thorndel.

Dulnear looked up toward the old man. In that

moment, his greatest desire was strangely to alleviate the elder's agony. "I am very sorry for the pain I have caused you," he said sincerely.

Shenndel looked at the warrior, frowning. The lines of age seemed to deepen as he stared. "Perhaps, but not nearly as sorry as you will be tomorrow," he said. He then went back into the house and snuffed out his lantern.

Dulnear dreamed that he was tied to a tree in a broad, open meadow. The grass was tall and lush, and burly oak trees grew thick around its borders. Surrounding him was a crowd of his countrymen, both young and old alike. They looked at him as a mob would stare at a convicted criminal waiting for his execution. He was naked, and unable to set himself free. Though he was dreaming, he felt the same shame and humiliation as if the scene playing out before him was really unfolding. The comfort of a sword, and the concealment of his long fur coat, were nowhere in sight, and the faces of onlookers were filled with disgust and contempt. Some of the northerners laughed, and others jeered as he desperately struggled to escape from his ropes.

As he scanned the crowd, he was surprised to see Faymia standing there with Son and Maren. She was holding Maren close, to keep the young girl's eyes shielded from his nakedness. Tears covered her cheeks, and she wept as one does at a funeral. The boy Son kept his eyes on the ground in front of him, as if ashamed to look upon the disgraced warrior.

Whipping his wrists back and forth and pulling with all of his might, Dulnear was overcome with desperation to be free. After several failed attempts, the despondent northerner began to call out to his friends for help. He filled his lungs with air and tried to shout, "Faymia!" but not a sound came out of his mouth. The feeling of desperation grew into panic, and again, he tried, "Faymia, Son, please help me!" but there was only silence, and the expressions on their faces showed no change.

Suddenly, there was a sound of thunder in the distance, and charcoal-gray clouds rolled over their heads like liquid misery. The sky opened up and began to pour bitterly cold rain. It felt like jagged stones pelting his body, and he knew that he would not make it if he remained exposed to the frigid shower. He called out to his friends for help again, and again his voice was absent. The looks on their faces told him that they could detect no attempt at communication from him at all, and it brought him more pain than if he would have been all alone.

The cold, wet crowd started to disperse, covering their heads and moving quickly toward a nearby road. Soon there were only his friends, watching and weeping as the mightiest man they knew was reduced to a shivering outcast, without honor, without his strength, and without the means to do anything about it. There was a flash of lightning, followed immediately by booming thunder, and the rain increased in cold and intensity. As the deluge poured, his friends also fled toward the road, leaving him all alone.

Dulnear was naked and abandoned in the truest sense. All that he had, and all that he was, was stripped away, and the feeling of vulnerability was more than he could bear. He attempted to pray, but he still had no voice. The cold penetrated every part of him, and he could scarce remember what it felt like to be warm. When there was nothing strong, or hopeful, or proud left inside of him, he wished only to die so that his anguish would end.

And then came the darkness.

"Wake up, Harbem!" Thorndel shouted.

Through the morning mist, Dulnear could see a small crowd of neighboring men gathered around a fire. It was situated near a wide tree stump just a few paces away. He assumed that his guard had diminished, since they were able to gather without waking him.

"How can you sleep so soundly hitched to a wagon?" Thorndel asked. "Especially on the eve of your execution."

Many sharp retorts came to Dulnear's mind. He usually enjoyed making comments that riled his enemies, but not today. He had slept through the night kneeling, and resting his shoulders against the yoke, with the weight of the cart preventing him from falling forward. Now he forced his stiff, aching legs to stand up. "Then it is to be execution," he observed.

"My father has not made his decision yet," the bitter man replied. "But I do not believe he would invite an audience here to watch him pardon you." He then paused, clenched his jaw, and added, "And know this; if he does pardon you, I will come for you, and you will die."

Though Thorndel was brash and reckless, Dulnear knew that he would still be a challenge for him. Like his brother, Tromdel, the man seemed to thrive on conflict. He remained silent. His heart was heavy, and he questioned his decision to come here. A feeling of great uncertainty came over him, and he wondered if there truly was life on the other side of death. The thought of having no conscious existence terrified him, and he began to pray quietly under his breath.

Thorndel looked as if he was about to say something else when his father emerged from the house. The old man was dressed, and armed, and his hair and beard had been combed. He walked over to Dulnear and Thorndel, and addressed the nearby group of northerners. "Countrymen," he began in a sour, tired tone. "The son of Athnear has returned to Tuas-arum. For generations, his family has looked down on us from their grand estate, thinking they are so much better than the rest of us. For years, they reigned undefeated in battle, and the hands of our kinsmen were proudly displayed throughout their home."

To Dulnear, it seemed as if the world around him was spinning. His head felt like it was on fire and his knees barely held his weight. He heard the words being spoken but they sounded distant, as if in a dream. Though they were the words he had traveled for weeks to hear, he struggled to maintain his concentration on them.

Shenndel continued, "This poltroon fancied himself above our way of life and fled to the south. He claims there is a better way, but none exists that carries any honor or glory!" The man's passionate words about the way of the north elicited applause from his friends, and he gave a dignified smile before he went on. "My son Tromdel sought him out. He tried to get him to come back but he was impaled for his effort."

Dulnear interrupted, pleading, "That is not true! He stole my Cre-dreact! He sought a death duel!"

"Silence!" Thorndel shouted, punching Dulnear in the face. He then smirked at the bound warrior before returning his attention to his father.

"It is true that he came here of his own accord," Shenndel explained. "He claimed his desire was to make restitution."

Through the surreal oration of the broken father's decision and the throbbing pain from Thorndel's fist, Dulnear labored to focus his thoughts toward his prayers to the Great Father. He prayed for the strength to die well. He prayed that his death would not be for nothing. He prayed for the safety of his friends in Laor, and for Faymia. And he prayed that other northerners would grow a distaste for their violent culture.

Shenndel went on, "Unhitch him from the wagon but leave him in the yoke."

As Thorndel did as he was told, Dulnear began to feel a sense of relief. He knew that it would be difficult to lose his head with a yoke around his neck. He looked at the men gathered around the fire and thought that perhaps they were there to form a gauntlet for him to endure. *I can take what these men can dole out*, he thought to himself. *I will recover.*

"When I think of what happened to my eldest son, I am weighed by a sense of shame," the old man said. "This man has brought humiliation upon my entire family. However, if I take his life, none of his family would feel the shame I have felt, for he is the last of his kin."

The words that Shenndel spoke caused the sense of

relief to evaporate as the penitent warrior imagined how he might be humiliated. The temptation to run gnawed at him, but he knew he wouldn't last long with a gang of angry northerners pursuing him, especially with a heavy yoke around his neck. Besides, he was determined to do what must be done.

"Therefore, the son of Athnear shall be as a dead man living," the resentful father announced. "Take his right hand!"

The announcement shot through Dulnear's chest like a javelin. "No!" he yelled. "Kill me!"

Thorndel grabbed the yoke that was secured around the pleading warrior's neck. There was a moment of struggle, and then several of the other northerners came to help drag him over to the nearby tree stump. They beat him as they pulled and yanked at the yoke, almost breaking his neck. When they had him at the stump, they ran his head into the side of it, taking the fight out of the man.

As Dulnear slumped over the edge of the tree stump, Thorndel gleefully grabbed his wrist and stretched it across while another man pulled back the sleeve of his fur coat. Again, the beaten man struggled, but the other northerners made it impossible to escape.

When Shenndel walked over to them, he already had his sword drawn. He dragged the blade across the exposed wrist and declared, "This will be my finest trophy. And you, Daeultu, shall be scorned and despised for the rest of your days." He then flashed a spiteful grin at the warrior, accompanied by a low growl.

"Please," was all that Dulnear could whisper before

he felt a quick jerking motion below his wrist and heard the roaring applause of the men all around him. He then felt himself being carried, and then tossed to the ground. From the corner of his eye, he could see his hand being held aloft by the old man. There was blood splattered across his white beard, and he cackled blithely. The warrior smelled something like burning flesh, then felt searing pain enveloping his arm. A couple of the invited guests were holding the fresh wound to the fire, cauterizing it so that he wouldn't bleed to death.

"That is it!" Shenndel yelled. "We would not want him to die now!"

Thorndel was laughing triumphantly nearby, and Dulnear could hear his own arm sizzling in the fire. Finally, the men pulled the arm out and dragged him back over toward the stump.

The old man and his son continued to gloat, and the whole earth felt like it was a small boat on an angry ocean. Finally, mercifully, Dulnear lost sight and sound of everything around him and slipped into unconsciousness.

Cold water splashed across Dulnear's face. He was only unconscious for a moment but, in his condition, it felt like hours. As the world around him slowly materialized from darkness and silence, the awareness of great pain through his arm and head emerged. Like a demonic drumbeat, the ache throbbed with each pulse of his heart. Through the celebration and revelry, he heard Shenndel order, "Take this refuse off of my land! He is a one-handed Nairetu, and it is shameful to even be in his presence!" The wounded warrior felt someone assisting him to his knees. As he moved, the agony increased, and he strained to hold onto his consciousness. When he opened his eyes, he saw Brunnlyn tucking his head under his left arm, helping him to his feet. "That is right," the old man continued. "Take him back to his estate, where his many trophies will remind him of his loss. The great Dulnear is nothing more than an object of ridicule now!" He then roared with laughter as his companions raised their mugs and drank to his malicious statement.

As the men laughed and cheered, Dulnear made his way down the path and to the road, with the help of Thorndel's cousin. He was in shock and exhausted, and the whole matter was made more difficult since he was still attached to the yoke. The wooden device felt much heavier now, and it seemed to be digging into his neck, exacerbating his condition.

When they reached the road and were no longer in sight of the assembly of revelers, Brunnlyn urged Dulnear to sit down for a moment. Wearily, the warrior sat, and Tromdel's cousin carefully removed the yoke from his shoulders. When he was done he crouched down, looked Dulnear squarely in the eyes and asked, "Why did you not kill Thorndel and me when you had the chance?"

Still in an agonizing fog, Dulnear thought for a moment, then answered, "I am tired of killing." His voice was weak, and he tried to swallow but his mouth was dry. He continued, "There is a better way than fighting and killing, and it cannot be found with more fighting and killing. I am so convinced of this that I was willing to go to the axe if it meant a little more peace in Aun."

"But what of your honor?" Brunnlyn asked. "You have never been defeated in battle."

The one-handed warrior emitted a weak laugh at the thought of the northern idea of honor. "There is a higher honor than that of dominance in combat," he explained. "There is a dignity in mercy, and fulfillment in peace. When I saw all of the trophies in my home last night, I felt only shame."

Brunnlyn rubbed the back of his neck. He began to speak, but cut himself short. After a moment, he said, "You should not return to your estate. Thorndel means to take it from you, and your head as well."

Dulnear released a weary exhale. "But I am already worse than dead," he lamented.

"I know," the fair-haired northerner replied. "But my cousin is a killer without sense. He cares not for fairness, only the thrill of ending lives."

"Then I have failed in my purpose for coming here," Dulnear replied.

Brunnlyn pressed his lips together and his eyebrows pressed inward. "Perhaps not," he said. "But you must get away from here. Go back down the road toward your home, but do not stop there. Head south again, and never return to the north." He then carefully helped the man to his feet and watched him walk until he was out of sight.

The pain and fatigue were great, and the one-handed man from the north fought to stay on his feet as the unbearable rhythm continued in his arm and head. He had lost his hand, but it was as if the heart was torn from his chest, and nothing remained but a great emptiness. His greatest desire was simply to lay down and die. As he walked, his body felt increasingly weighed down by the regret of his decision to make restitution for the death of Tromdel. *It would have been easier just to let the brute kill me. I am a fool*, he thought to himself.

Bloodied, burned, and beaten, Dulnear slowly continued his arduous journey down the road, occasionally stumbling from dizziness and the excruciating pain that refused to relent. Willing himself to stay on his feet, he looked up, and could see someone in the road ahead of him. There stood Faymia, waiting for him.

CHAPTER ELEVEN
An Empty Chest

DULNEAR STOOD IN PAIN-FILLED BEWILDER-MENT at the sight of his friend. He looked at Faymia, feeling equal parts relief and shame. He carried a great fondness for her, but was no longer the warrior she knew the day before.

"Dulnear!" she cried as she ran toward him. "You made it!"

The man stood and looked into the face of the woman. Tears began to pool in the corners of his eyes. "I failed," he lamented, and his knees gave out. He fell to the ground and began to weep. "It was all for naught. I have lost everything and gained nothing. Tromdel's brother still seeks my death, and I am a Nairetu now, worse than dead. My hand has been taken from me, and I can no longer wield a sword."

Weeping along with the sobbing northerner, Faymia reached out, lifted his chin, and looked into his eyes. Her forehead wrinkled with concern. "What can I do?" she asked.

"Leave me," Dulnear said, trembling. "I will only bring you misery. I will return to my home. There, Thorndel can complete his revenge by ending my life and claiming my estate. It is the only way that you, and the children in Laor, will ever be safe."

Beneath the tears, an amused expression crept over Faymia's face. She held her gaze on Dulnear's eyes and asked softly, "Is anyone ever truly safe?" Then she added, "You cannot protect everyone all of the time, my precious. Besides, I have already gone through the dread of losing you once, and I don't think I could do it again."

Dulnear lowered his head. The pain and shock of the last few hours made it difficult to think clearly. He waited until his tears subsided, and then pulled himself up off of the ground. Finally, standing there, he admitted, "I do not know what to do."

The woman reached up and wiped away some of the blood that was drying on her friend's face. She then gently lifted his arm, pushed back the sleeve of his coat, and examined the blackened wound where his hand had been removed. "Let's start by dressing these wounds," she said.

The man exhaled deeply. He trusted the woman and said, "I have supplies at my home, but we must be fast. If Thorndel finds us there, he will kill us both."

"Okay, are you sure you can make it there quickly?" Faymia asked with a concerned expression.

"I have to," Dulnear assured as he began walking toward his estate. Each step was painful, and it was difficult to summon the will to continue, but having his friend with him brought a measure of fortitude.

When they arrived, they entered through the eastern kitchen door. The kitchen was a large room with an ample roasting range to one side, and in the center of the room was a long wooden table with benches situated on each side of it. Being in the house during daylight had a different feel to it than the night before. Windows allowed light to illuminate the room. A layer of dust could be seen covering everything, and cobwebs were plentiful.

While Faymia ran back outside to fetch water from the well, Dulnear sat at the end of the table and waited. It had been a long time since he had sat at the kitchen table. It reminded him of times during his boyhood when he snuck mid-afternoon snacks while his father was busy working. Even though growing up in the north was difficult, there were still times in his childhood that he remembered fondly, and when he thought about them, it made him sad that they were gone forever.

When Faymia returned with clean water, she helped her friend remove his long fur coat and gently cleaned his wounds. The sensation of cold water on burned flesh was foreign and unpleasant. As it mingled with the black marks on his skin it flowed onto the floor, leaving puddles of dark-tinged water. Dulnear told her where she could find clean linens with which to dress the wounds. She rushed off to get them, and made sure to take enough to make extra dressings if they were needed during their journey south.

When she came back, she lightly wrapped his arm, occasionally wincing at the sight of the painful-looking injury. When she was finished caring for him, she took his hand and helped him stand up. She then put her hands around his waist and slid his sword belt so that he could reach the hilt with his left hand. "You never know," she said with an awkward smile.

Dulnear suppressed a grin. He was amused by her gesture, but the sadness smothered his amusement. Suddenly, he remembered something. "Faymia!" he said urgently. "We have to—" Just then, the sound of drunken men carrying on outside the house could be heard. He threw on his coat, crouched down, and peered out the window to see the revelers that had been gathered at Shenndel's estate. "We have to get out of here!" he whispered.

There was a noise at the kitchen door and the pair froze. Then the sound of Thorndel's voice could be heard, shouting, "No, the other door!" Dulnear and Faymia stood frozen as they heard the other rear entrance to the house open. A gang of carousing northerners poured into the narrow hall adjacent to the kitchen. It sounded like a parade of tipsy buffoons laughing and talking about how disgusted they were by the size of the home. "He is probably wallowing in the drawing room," someone said, and they began to make their way down the hall and up the stairs.

Dulnear felt violated by the invasion of ne'er-do-wells. He wished for the strength to confront them, but that desire was immediately eclipsed by the contempt he felt for his current condition. He breathed deeply and instructed, "We will make for the tree line at the southern edge of the property."

After briefly checking for stragglers, they ran toward the outbuilding that housed the yoke and wagon that Dulnear pulled to Shenndel's house. Hiding behind the building, Dulnear hoped that they could make it across his land before Thorndel or any of his friends noticed them. There was plenty of daylight, and he was counting on the party to be too drunk to notice any movement from outside the house. When they were confident that they had not been seen they dashed further, to a large oak tree. Hiding behind the oak, the man from the north gave a sad chuckle.

"What is it?" Faymia asked.

"Just a memory," the large man explained. "Remind me sometime to tell you about the time I tricked my brother into jumping out of this tree."

The woman's eyebrows raised and a bemused smile crept across her face. "You can bet I will," she said.

Returning to the urgency of the moment, Dulnear said, "There is another cluster of trees a short distance from here. Once we reach it, we should be out of view from the house. If we are fortunate, they will have moved on from the drawing room, and are searching for me on the third floor."

The two sprinted to the group of trees unseen. Once there, Dulnear explained, "We can travel back the way we came. Once we reach the river, we will walk west until we reach the Contuent Bridge. Hopefully Thorndel will be too drunk—or too lazy—to follow through with his threat."

The two traveled south through woods and fields. At first, every scurrying creature and every random sound set Faymia on edge. She dreaded waking one morning to an ambush of northerners, especially after her experience with the Malitae. Eventually, she grew in the confidence that there didn't seem to be anyone following them. They made camp every night, as they always did, but Faymia did the hunting and cooking while Dulnear rested. She was concerned for him, and continually kept an eye on him as she performed camp chores. He did very little talking, and spent most nights staring into the fire as if his mind was elsewhere.

One night, as they sat across the campfire from each other, she asked, "Where will we go once we cross the Fuar?"

As if awoken from a trance, the man answered, "There is a farm outside of Blackcloth. My friend Aesef is there. He is both kind and wise, and I would very much like to see him."

Curious about how a warrior from the north was acquainted with a farmer from the south, she asked, "How do you know this farmer?"

"I helped him get rid of some unwanted company," he answered. Then he stared into the fire for a moment before continuing, "It is where I killed Tromdel. He stole something very valuable to me in order to draw me into a confrontation. It was my Cre-dreact, the sword that my father used to train me as a lad. He joined in with some southern hoodlums and they made their camp on Aesef's land. During our battle, he attacked the boy I was protecting, and I ended his life." He then laid down and pulled his coat around his neck.

Faymia moved closer to Dulnear. She wished that she could take his pain and release him from the grip of anguish and regret. "How did you come to be acquainted with the boy?" she asked.

The large man's expression changed as he began talking

about the boy. He looked wistful and began, "I had just left my home to explore the southern lands by foot. I was hoping to make a more peaceful life for myself. One day, as I was dining in a pub, the boy Son walked in, hoping to fill his canteen. A good-for-nothing man bullied and robbed him. He was alone, and had no one to stand up for him. His father abandoned him, and his mother was lost to insanity. It seemed wrong not to involve myself. I protected him, taught him to use a sword, and about courage, and fortitude. I am as proud of him as a person could be." As a tear ran down his temple, he added, "He is like my own, and I made this journey for his protection."

"And what about the girl Maren?" she asked.

Dulnear smiled as another tear fell, and answered, "Son and I found her orphaned when her mother and father died on the road to Blackcloth. The boy insisted that we take her in. She is quirky, and lovely, and I fear that one day she will get lost in a storybook and never come back."

Faymia smiled. She felt close to the man as he shared about the children. She hoped to one day see them together and be a part of their lives. "Do you think you'll see them again?" she asked.

"I do hope so, but I really don't know," he answered. "If I was confident that Thorndel would not track me, I would definitely say yes. No other northerner would ever bother with me because there is no honor in killing a Nairetu. But Thorndel is different. He seems to care not for honor or esteem, only revenge, even though I have already made restitution." He then closed his eyes, pulled his coat closed a little tighter, and began to shiver. "I have already made restitution," he repeated to himself. Then, trailing off, he whispered, "I do not understand."

The woman was troubled. Dulnear traveled most of the way to Tuas-arum without ever seeming to care much about the cold, and now he was shaking. She touched his forehead. He was burning up with fever. She said a prayer and watched him until he was sound asleep. Eventually, though she was gripped with uneasiness, she drifted off into a dreamless sleep.

After traveling through the thick northern woods, the two reached the Fuar River. Its frigid, raging current and abundant mist was a reminder of their narrow escape from the Malitae. They traveled westward along its bank, stopping often to rest and retreat into the woods to allow themselves a break from the relentless moisture. It was slow going, as Dulnear's condition seemed to worsen each day. Eventually, the Contuent Bridge came into view, and they were able to cross into southern Aun.

Once out of the north, they began walking west until they reached the road that led southward toward Blackcloth. It was a well-worn path that was surrounded by dense forest to the west and open fields, lush with tall grass, to the east. From where the two roads met, they could see a great distance and Dulnear walked along, his eyes surveying the landscape.

After traveling south for a while, the man from the north spotted a large, moss-covered tree trunk that had fallen near the road. "I need to rest for a moment," he stated, and sat on the log as he looked out over the eastern fields. The sky was its usual heavy curtain of gray, and the wind seemed uncertain as it shifted in intensity with each passing moment, whipping his hair against his pale face.

Faymia sat down at his left, and asked, "Are you okay?"

He didn't answer but continued to stare into the horizon, his head slightly rocking back and forth as if it had become heavier from their journey south. The great sadness and fever that soaked him drained all of his strength.

As the two looked out into the sky together, the wind kicked up and began to push the clouds northerly like a mighty, invisible hand. Fingers of late afternoon sunlight broke through the gray ceiling and danced across the fields. It was a rarely seen display in the usually dismal Aun, and something in the man from the north longed to take in the golden luminance like a thirsty tree. The defeated warrior and the spent slave woman held hands and watched in engrossment until the waltzing sunlight retreated up to the heavens and the gray clouds returned.

When Dulnear turned his attention toward Faymia, he noticed that her cheek was streaked with tears. He squeezed her hand gently, and wanted to ask about them, but instead just watched the last teardrop hang from her chin until it let go and fell onto her cloak. Finally, he said, "Perhaps we should be on our way," and the two moved slowly toward Blackcloth, hand in hand.

Later that day, the two approached a village. It was small but bustling with activity as they walked the road that brought them from one end of the town to the other.

There was a pub and a few shops that had a steady flow of people coming and going. Occasionally, someone would give the travelers a second glance, and Faymia would do her best to keep her nerves calm. It was the first time they had seen a village since stopping to purchase new clothes for the woman and it made her uncomfortable to be there. If there were any associates of Tcharron there, word was sure to get back to him that she was still alive, and Dulnear was in no condition to protect her.

Despite being hungry and tired, they did not stop but continued on until they found a place to camp for the night. It was well hidden from the road and contained a small area of flat ground surrounded by large stones and fallen trees. The man from the north was pale and weak, and had very little to say. Concerned, the woman continued to take on the chores of building a fire, catching rabbit, and cooking dinner so that he could rest.

She forced two forked sticks into the ground and removed the bark from a third stick to make a spit to roast the rabbit over. When the rabbit was ready to eat, Dulnear was already sound asleep. Faymia decided to let him sleep, but left some meat for him on the spit in case he woke up hungry later in the night. When she had finished eating, she tossed the inedible parts of the game deeper into the woods and prepared a place to lie down near her friend.

She laid down on her back, wrapped in her cloak, and stared into the somber night sky. She listened to the sick warrior's breathing. It was much louder and heavier than was usual for him. She said a prayer and hoped he would be feeling better in the morning, but it did little to set her mind at ease.

Hours later, she was still awake, haunted by fears of losing her friend and the freedom she longed to keep. When she did eventually fall asleep, it was restless and fitful.

The next morning, Faymia woke to the sound of voices. She sat up quickly and looked around. Hearing footsteps and commotion from the direction of the road, she remained still and listened intently. As the sound of the people on the road faded into the distance, she was relieved that the fire was no longer smoldering, and that their camp was well hidden.

When she got up, she discovered that the rabbit she had left on the spit was still there, untouched, and Dulnear was still sleeping. She went to check on him, and found that he was trembling, and his face was hot. She carefully pulled back the sleeve of his coat, removed the dressing, and saw that the wound at the end of his arm was oozing a green substance, and the area around it was red and swollen.

She gently replaced the bandage and searched the inside of the man's bag for something that would help. There, she found a leather pouch filled with coins, and placed it in her own bag. She then dragged some fallen tree limbs near where her friend was sleeping, and did what she could to make sure that their campsite was even more difficult to see from the road than before.

She was going to have to leave Dulnear alone, and the thought of that frightened her. Her friend, whom she had great fondness for, was unable to care for or protect himself. He would be completely vulnerable if Thorndel tracked them there. Also, she was going to have to return to the village they passed through the day before. Her plan was to get what she needed, return to the man quickly, and hope for the best.

Faymia hid her bow and arrows but kept her sword with her, under her cloak. She kissed her friend on the forehead, said another prayer, and walked quickly back in the direction of the village.

When Faymia entered the village, she headed straight for the pub. It was a busy place filled with chattering patrons who were putting off more productive activities for a morning brew. She disliked being there. The familiar smell of smoke and ale stirred memories in her that she would rather forget. Fortunately, it was still early enough in the day that most of the patrons were still sober.

She approached the barkeep, who was wiping down the counter, and politely asked, "Excuse me, can you please tell me where I can buy some medicine?"

From behind the bar, the stocky, unkempt man replied rudely, "Excuse me, but do I look like the town answer man?" He then placed an empty mug upon the bar and waited for her to reply.

Faymia had forgotten how men treated her when Dulnear was not at her side. She fought back the desire to say something disrespectful, knowing that the wisest thing was to draw as little attention to herself as possible. "I'm sorry," she said. "I'll have a mug of stout. Here, you may keep the change," and she placed a coin from Dulnear's leather pouch on the bar.

The barkeep filled the mug for her, took the money, and gave her a crooked smile. "There's an apothecary who lives up the westward path at the southern edge of town. He's not home much, but you can give him a try," he said as he toweled off a freshly washed stein. "What do you need him for?"

The woman ignored the barkeep's question, quickly took a considerable gulp of the stout, and replied, "Thank you for your help," before jogging out the door.

She dashed to the southern edge of the village, finding the westward path. It was narrow, and winding, and led up a high hill. It had few homes along it, and the woman hoped that it wasn't going to be a long hike. She wasn't exactly sure what she was looking for, only that she was mostly confident that she'd know it when she found it.

Eventually, she came to a small thatched cottage on the right side of the path. The garden was unkempt and littered with odds and ends that she couldn't identify. She almost kept walking but was startled when, from inside the house, there was the sound of an angry donkey. There was a loud, "Hee-haw!" and suddenly the front door was shattered from the inside. Immediately, the newly freed beast came running out. She gasped as it ran straight toward her and brayed noisily. It stopped just an arm's length in front of her, then sat down and sniffed the air as if expecting something. Frozen in a state of shock and amusement, Faymia stood there wide-eyed, wondering if she should back away.

"Never mind him," a voice called from the porch. "He didn't like the smell of his lungworm medicine. Are ye lost?"

Faymia looked toward the doorway where a freckled old man stood. He stood about her height and, though the top of his head was bald, he had the most amusing combover padded with curly, white hair. "Are you the apothecary?" she asked.

"At yer service," he answered with an awkward smile. "What can I do for ye?"

"I have a sick friend," she began, the urgency returning to her. "He has a severe burn. I think it's infected. He's burning with fever."

The kindly man pushed his lips together and squinted. Rubbing his chin, he said, "Why don't ye come in. I'll see what I can find." Then he turned and slowly made his way back into the house.

Faymia followed him, stepping over pieces of broken door and wishing that he would move faster. There was a thin layer of smoke in the air, and the combined smells of oils and ointments was almost more than she could bear. The walls were lined with shelves stocked with jars of all shapes and sizes. There was a large table in the center of the front room where the apothecary had been mixing dried herbs of varying shades of green and yellow. There was also an oil lamp, and she could see black marks on the table where there had clearly been an accident or two. She wondered why the donkey was inside the house but, before she could give it much thought, her contemplation was interrupted by the old man.

"Now, a bad burn, ye say?" the apothecary asked as he searched among the many jars along the wall and continued to rub his whiskery chin.

"Yessir," she answered. "Actually, his hand was removed, and his arm placed in the fire."

"You don't say!" the man responded. "Is he a soldier? There hasn't been a war around here fer quite some time."

"He's from the north," she answered. It was more information than she cared to give, but there was something about the old man she felt she could trust.

"Oh, I see," he said. "There's always fighting in the north. Never seems to stop. Violent people up there." He then took down a small jar of a gooey green and gray substance. When he removed the lid, a putrid odor mingled with the other scents in the air. "This should help the burn," he stated as he sniffed the jar and wrinkled his nose.

Faymia gagged. "What is that?"

"Snail slime," the old man explained. "Spread this on the burn before putting on fresh bandages. It will ease the pain, and keep the wound from getting worse." He replaced the lid, handed her the jar, then walked over to the opposite wall where dried leaves and flowers filled the shelves from floor to ceiling. "Okay, now what do I have for a fever?" he thought to himself aloud. He finally stood on his toes, reached high, and pulled down a jar of small dried leaves. "Here we go, coriander. Make a tea from this as often as he'll drink it," he said as he handed her the jar.

"Thank you very much, sir," the woman said as she pulled a coin from the leather pouch.

"You're most welcome," the apothecary said with a smile as he pocketed the coin. "Is there anything else you'll be needin' today?"

Faymia cleared her throat and swallowed. Nervously, she asked, "How much for the mule?"

Faymia quickly made her way back to the campsite. She had already been gone for the entire morning, and her concern for the man from the north was playing with her imagination. When she arrived, Dulnear was asleep. The remaining rabbit looked as if it had been nibbled at but most of it was still on the spit. After she tied up the mule, she knelt by the man's side and gently attempted to wake him up. It took several tries until he finally opened his eyes in a feverish stupor.

"You came back," he said with a weak voice. "I thought you took my money and left me."

The statement took Faymia by surprise but she shrugged it off. "I'm afraid it will take more than a fever and a stinky arm to get rid of me," she retorted. "Now, try to sit up so I can take care of this burn." She then helped him sit up and cautiously slid the coat off of his right arm. It was no easy task, since the giant man's upper body swayed back and forth like a tall, dead tree in an angry wind. When she removed the bandage, the smell was worse than before, and she hid her reaction so that he would not become discouraged.

"What is that horrible odor?" the man asked.

"It's okay. I just need to clean something up," she answered. "Can you sit up for a moment while I warm some water?"

"I reckon so," he said as he continued to sway precariously.

The woman took a coffee pot from Dulnear's bag and emptied her canteen into it. She quickly got the fire going again and started to heat up the water. Once it was hot enough, she used some of it to wash his wound, and saved the rest to make the tea with.

As she opened the jar that the apothecary sold her, she said, "This isn't going to smell very good, but it will heal the burn." She then carefully applied the snail ointment to the end of his arm.

"But you just got rid of the other stench," the man said, almost asleep while sitting up.

She then put a fresh dressing on the wound and assisted him to ease his arm back into his coat. Then she prepared the coriander tea and urged him to take a few sips of it before he became too weak to sit up any longer.

She gave him some time to rest, then helped him drink the remainder of the tea. Eventually, she managed to get him off the ground and onto the donkey. He laid on his stomach across the animal's back. He was so large that only his trunk fit on its back and his feet dragged along the ground on both sides.

Once Faymia had her friend secured on the mule, she packed up their belongings, removed any signs that they had been there, and headed towards Blackcloth.

CHAPTER TWELVE
REUNIONS AND REVELATIONS

ULNEAR AWOKE, BUT HIS EYELIDS were too heavy to open. He was lying in a bed, and the scent of his surroundings was familiar. For a moment, he thought he might still be sleeping and that his sense of consciousness was just another dream. When he finally managed to open his eyes, he was startled. Hovering next to his bed was a small, dark-haired girl with an expressionless face, and she was staring intently at the resting giant.

"Good morning," she whispered, with eyes growing wider.

Realizing who the face belonged to, Dulnear exhaled with relief. "Maren!" he exclaimed. "Where am I? How did you get here?"

"By horse," she answered, then hugged the man and ran out of the room.

As the sound of the girl's footsteps trailed off, the world around Dulnear began to come into focus. He realized that he was in one of the guest rooms of his friend Aesef's house. He didn't know how Faymia managed to get him there, but he was glad that she did. He reckoned the old farmer must have sent his servant, Phel, to Laor to collect Son and Maren.

While he was still gathering his thoughts, another voice spoke. "You're awake!" The boy Son stood in the doorway, beaming. His cheeks were rosy, and his blonde hair was blown in every direction.

"It is you!" the man from the north replied happily. "I almost did not recognize your voice! It is deeper, and you are taller."

The boy said nothing, but instead went to the edge of the bed, wrapped his arms around his friend's neck, and squeezed as hard as he could. Dulnear reached up and embraced Son, and the two began to weep together.

Through his tears, the boy declared, "I thought I'd never see you again."

"Me too," Dulnear sniffled. "And I wish that I had good news for you, but I am afraid I failed at my purpose for leaving you in the first place."

Son stood straight and wiped his tears on his coat sleeve. "What do you mean?" he asked.

The man from the north felt a weight on his chest. He hated giving a bad report to his friend after being reunited. He took a deep breath. "I meant to make restitution, to end the cycle of revenge," he explained. "They took my right hand, a humiliation worse than death to my people. My debt to Tromdel's family should be considered paid, but Tromdel's brother still wants to kill me."

Son sat on the edge of the bed, his forehead wrinkled with concern for the circumstance his mentor and friend found himself in. "If he finds you, and you defeat him, will others come for you?" he asked.

Dulnear thought for a moment, then answered, "I suppose not. There is no glory in slaying a one-handed man, and too much shame in being defeated by one. Thorndel cares not for honor or glory, only for taking the lives of those who bruise his fragile pride."

A look of relief grew on Son's face as he said, "Then all you have to do is defeat him and it's over."

The man had no desire to squelch the boy's hopes, but his own faith was at its lowest. "Son, I am not the warrior you knew before," he said. "I am afraid that I am no match for Thorndel left-handed. I am not even sure I could beat Maren."

The boy sat silent for a moment. He then swallowed and began, "We'll find a way together. I've already had to say goodbye to you once, and I don't want to do it again."

The man from the north found little encouragement in his friend's words. As far as he was concerned, he died in Tuas-arum when Shenndel took his hand. He didn't want to let the boy down, but he was certain he'd be leaving him again, for his own protection. "I suppose time will tell," he murmured.

Son replied, "Dulnear, you once told me that evil men prevail when good people choose to avoid conflict. We have to believe that—" and he was cut off by another voice at the bedroom door.

"How are you feeling?" Faymia asked.

The broken man looked up at her. He was taken aback by her lovely appearance. She had bathed, and her clothes had been washed and mended. Her raven hair had been braided along her temples, and her eyes looked bright and full of life. For a brief moment his discouragement lifted and his heart beat stronger. He asked, "Faymia, how did you get me here?"

"I purchased a mule and he carried you. He's strong, and stubborn, like you!" she explained. "He was a great help, but it wasn't easy getting him through the dead forest north of here."

"The dead forest? Why did you travel through the forest?" he asked.

"I discovered that I was sharing the road with a slaver caravan," she said. "I'll tell you all about it when you're feeling better."

"I look forward to hearing every detail," Dulnear said. "I take it you have met Son and Maren then."

"Oh yes," Faymia smiled. She looked at Son. "He is quite the impressive young man. He's been working very hard on something in the barn, and when he's here in the house, he keeps a close eye on you. We have to remind him to eat and sleep when he needs to."

Son blushed. "And when I'm in the barn, I have Maren watching you in here."

"I noticed," the man from the north said. "She nearly frightened me to death when I awoke."

Son laughed. "It takes some getting used to. She has taken to waking me that way every morning."

"Speaking of Maren, she braided my hair," the woman added. "What do you think?"

"It is lovely," Dulnear grinned.

Son, looking slightly embarrassed, stood up. "I'll let Aesef know that you're awake," he said. "I'm sure he'd like to come and see you." He then smiled at the two and jaunted off down the hall.

"Your friends really love you," Faymia observed as she took Son's place at the edge of the bed.

The woman's smile gave the man from the north strength. "And I them," he answered. "Thank you for getting me here. I am incredibly impressed, for I know it must not have been an easy task. What has become of this donkey that carried me?"

"I believe Maren has adopted the poor fellow," she answered. "She calls him Earl, and sits on him reading her books while he wanders around eating whatever he can find."

The man chuckled in amusement, recalling his experiences with the girl before returning to the north. "Well, I am glad she has made a friend," he joked as he rested his heavy head back onto the pillow.

Faymia's expression changed, as if a burden had been placed upon her shoulders. "Dulnear," she began. "Do you think that Thorndel will track us here to the farm?"

The small amount of strength Dulnear felt quickly faded. He answered somberly, "I do not know, but I cannot put my friends at risk. I have to assume that he is coming, and act upon that."

"But you have to fully recover. You are in no condition to travel," his friend advised.

Dulnear drew a deep breath. "All right, I shall stay a little while longer," he said. "But then I have to say goodbye again. You may join me if you wish, or you can stay. I want only to keep Tromdel's brother as far away from the children as possible."

Faymia examined her friend's face. It had always been the face of one who had endured, grown, and pondered much. It was one of sadness, and strength, caring and cunning. But today there was something different about it. It had a vacant quality. She finally answered, "I want to be with you, Dulnear. It would probably be the best way to avoid being found by Tcharron anyway."

The man from the north reached for the woman's hand, held it gently, and closed his eyes. Still in pain, and weak, he felt his surroundings begin to fade as he drifted back into a woozy sleep.

It was late in the afternoon, and the light coming through Dulnear's window was growing dim. Down the hall was the dining room, and he woke to the sound of the children chatting and setting the table. He remembered the meals he'd shared with them before and missed those times. Unfortunately, in the condition he was in, he felt more like hiding in his room than joining them for dinner. Just then, he heard heavy footsteps approach his door, and then it slowly swung open. A short, round, gray-haired old man stood there. It was Aesef.

"Hello there, Dulnear," the man said cheerily through his long white beard.

The man from the north was grateful that his friend never seemed worried or ruffled. His consistently pleasant disposition was a comfort to him. "Aesef," he welcomed. "Come in. It is good to see you!"

"You're looking much better," the old farmer said as he pulled a chair next to the bed and sat down. "You had me quite concerned when you arrived."

"Thank you. And thank you again for your hospitality," Dulnear replied.

"It's my pleasure," his friend said. "You and the children, and the lady Faymia, are always welcome here."

The man thought for a moment and asked, "I'm curious; why did you bring the children here?"

Aesef smiled warmly and answered slowly, "Because, when you're suffering, going through crisis, or encountering great loss, having family at your side has a way of easing the burden."

"I appreciate that," he answered. "Their faces are like medicine to me."

"They are good for me too. Now, how is that wound?" the kindly farmer asked as he gently placed his hand on the northerner's right arm.

Dulnear sat up, leaned his back against the headboard of the bed, and slowly held out his arm to be examined. Aesef carefully removed the bandage, revealing a badly scarred stump where a powerful hand once had been. The infection had cleared up, and what remained was skin that looked much like pink and red melted wax from the end of his arm to almost halfway to his elbow. It was the first time the man from the north had really taken a good look at the wound. As he rotated his forearm in front of his eyes, his heart sank even deeper as the reality of losing his hand was laid naked.

"I would say that it's healing nicely," the farmer mentioned as he opened a small jar, and lightly applied a fresh layer of snail ointment to the burn. "The searing could have been done in a far less clumsy fashion, but it probably saved your life."

Dulnear sneered, "It is a northern bad joke meant to keep me alive after taking away my life."

"Take away your life?" Aesef asked as he put new bandages over the burn. "Are you not more than a hand?"

"I am a warrior," he answered. "I cannot wield a sword without my right hand. I cannot defend those I care for. The children need a warrior. Faymia needs a warrior. I was regarded as one of the greatest in the north, and now I cannot even defend myself!"

"Yes, you are a warrior," his friend agreed. He then tilted his head and asked, "But what else are you?"

"I do not understand your question," Dulnear admitted.

"I mean that, surely, when the Great Father created you, he had more in mind for you than simply swinging a sword," the farmer explained.

"The Great Father has abandoned me," the man from the north huffed. "I wanted to do what was virtuous, what was right. I was willing to lay down my life for my friends, and now I am the laughingstock of Tuas-arum!"

"I understand," Aesef assured. "But you can't expect things to go as you hope simply because you do what's right. For an act to truly be selfless, it's required of us to lay down our expectations."

Dulnear sat silently for a moment. He knew his friend was right, but the pain and feelings of abandonment weighed heavily upon his shoulders. "The most difficult part," he began, "was the silence."

"What do you mean?" his friend asked.

"I prayed for comfort, and received none," he said. "I asked for wisdom, and the Great Father kept his mouth shut. I begged for anything that would prove to me that he was the least bit concerned, and heard only the coldest silence in return."

"I'm very sorry you experienced that," Aesef consoled. "But I do not believe that the Great Father is ever silent unless he has a purpose for his silence." He then paused for a moment and added, "I have to disagree with you though. The Great Father did answer your prayers, with much love and generosity."

Dulnear couldn't believe what he'd just heard. He just looked at his friend with an expression that was part confusion and part offense. "You must be making a joke," he accused.

"Did he not send you a companion for your journey?" the old man asked. "Was she not a comfort, and a friend? Did she not rescue you when you were too sick to carry on? If ever there was an answer to your prayers, it was the gift of your friend Faymia. She was just as much an answer to your prayers as you were an answer to hers."

A small fracture began to form in Dulnear's wall of doubt. However, he found it very difficult to see worth in himself without the ability to hold a sword. His lip quivered as he asked, "But why did he allow me to lose my hand?"

Taking a deep breath, Aesef answered, "I don't know. But I know that there is a boy, and a little girl, that love you just as much without it. And I know that you are so much more than just a warrior."

"If not a warrior, then what am I?" he asked.

"To me, a friend," the farmer answered. "To Maren, a shield; to Son, a father; and to Faymia, one who sees her as she truly is. *Warrior* doesn't even come close to describing who you are, Dulnear. You are a miracle and a champion, and you wouldn't cease being a miracle and a champion if you lost your entire arm."

Dulnear's eyes swelled with tears as the man's words sank deep into his broken heart. "Thank you," he said as he wiped his cheek.

"You are not abandoned," his friend added. "You just haven't been able to see through the heaviness."

Just then, a beautiful sound could be heard from down the hall. The children and Faymia were singing a tune while Phel accompanied them on a stringed instrument. The man from the north closed his eyes and listened. As he did, more tears found their way down his face, and he contemplated the words of his friend. The crack in his wall of doubt grew bigger, and he asked, "Can I join you in the dining room tonight?"

"Of course," Aesef answered. "You are always welcome at my table."

Dulnear put on a robe that Aesef had placed in his room days ago, and he followed the farmer down the hall. When he sat at the table, his friends gathered around him, placed their hands on his shoulders, and lovingly prayed for the man who was a miracle to them. As they did, he felt the love of the Great Father pour through the opening in his wall of doubt, and he felt hope.

Days later, Dulnear and Son took a walk together. It felt refreshing for the man to be outside and stretch his legs. As they strolled across Aesef's fields of wheat and barley, they recalled their adventures together, and were even able to laugh at some of them. It was good medicine for his heart to see the boy smile and talk as if no time had passed since they were last together.

When they approached the ravine where Dulnear slew Tromdel and Son had almost died, they stopped at the edge and looked out over the blackened, twisted trees. It was quiet, and a gentle breeze stirred up the scent of wet earth and wild grass. "I see that life is returning to the scorched wood," the boy observed, breaking the silence.

Noticing the new growth on the opposite side of the ravine, the man from the north replied, "That it is." From where he stood, he could see the place where he'd ended the life of his fellow northerner. Feelings of melancholy washed over him, and he looked down at his handless arm.

Son watched his friend and mentor closely. "Are you okay?" he asked.

A sad smile crossed Dulnear's face. "I am trying to be," he answered honestly. "Not having my right hand is going to take some getting used to."

Son turned toward him and asked, "Remember when my mother died, and my father abandoned me?"

"Of course," the man answered. "I was there with you. Your heart was so broken."

"It was a terrible time, but I learned something through all of it," the boy said.

"And what did you learn?" Dulnear asked.

"I learned that sometimes the parts that are broken grow back stronger than before," Son said as he pointed toward his own chest, and then to Dulnear's arm. "It will get better."

The boy's words lifted some of the sadness, and the

man said, "Thank you. You really do seem stronger since I left Laor. What have you been doing with yourself?"

"Mostly tending the farm, and Maren," the boy said. "She isn't much for caring for herself. I think she'd starve to death if I didn't remind her to eat once in a while. She spends most of her time reading adventure books. I'm not even sure where she gets them!" He paused for a moment, then continued, "I also practice the fighting that you showed me, and I still like to create things out of wood and metal."

"And how are the crops?" the man from the north inquired.

"Enough to feed us," the boy answered. "And I sell my creations in the village. They are quite popular."

"That is great news. It sounds like you really have your hands full," Dulnear observed.

"I do. And what about you?" Son asked. "I know that things did not go well in Tuas-arum, but what about Faymia? How did she come to travel with you?"

The man from the north paused before answering. "I met her at a pub outside of Ahmcathare," he said, trying not to expose certain details.

The inquisitive boy pressed, "What was she doing there?"

"Well, she served my meal," he said, running his hand through his hair, and glancing away from the boy.

"She's a barmaid?" Son asked.

"Well, sort of," Dulnear replied.

"What do you mean?"

"She does other things too."

"Like cooking?"

"Sure," Dulnear said, hoping it was the end of the boy's questioning on the matter.

"It sounds like she has many skills. That's good," the lad observed.

"Yes," was all the man would say before resuming his walk.

The two began to make their way back to the house. Neither said anything until Son asked, "But how did she come to join you on your trip to Tuas-arum?"

The man stopped, closed his eyes, took a deep breath and answered, "She ran away from her slaver."

The boy's eyebrows raised and his eyes grew wide. "She's a slave?" he asked.

Frustrated yet amused by Son's persistent curiosity, Dulnear answered, "Yes, Son, and I nearly lost my life keeping her from being recaptured."

"Nearly lost your life?" the boy asked, the pitch of his voice getting higher.

"Her slaver recruited some warriors from the south, and they tracked us down near the Fuar River," he explained. "We had to jump into the water to escape."

"I can't believe it!" the boy exclaimed. Then his expression changed, and he asked, "Do you think they are still looking for her?"

"It is possible, but her slaver may think she is dead," the man answered.

"Even so, if she's recognized, it will not go well," Son observed, rubbing his chin.

"I know," Dulnear said, "and I'm in no condition to fight the slavers off."

"Is there anything else we can do?" the boy asked.

"She must be pretty important to you if you were willing to risk your life for her."

The man from the north contemplated as they walked. "I was going to help her…" he said before a sudden thought silenced him. The recollection of something rose up in his chest. He looked at his friend and declared, "Son, I have to go back to Tuas-arum!"

CHAPTER THIRTEEN
MAKES YOU STRONGER

ASEF'S MOUTH DROPPED OPEN AND he scratched his jaw. "Return to Tuas-arum?" he asked.

"Yes," the man from the north replied confidently before taking a sip of tea. The two sat at the end of the large dining table. Dulnear's sword was belted around his waist for the first time since arriving at the old farmer's house. "I need to collect something valuable from my estate."

"Dulnear, I don't think that's wise," the old man said. "You've only been on your feet for a short time. What if you happen to cross paths with Thorndel?"

The northerner searched for the right words to answer his friend's question but before he could, Son ran into the room carrying a long, heavy contraption. "I finished it!" he shouted as he enthusiastically presented it to his friend.

"What is it?" Dulnear asked with a curious smile.

The boy's eyes sparkled and a wide grin covered his face. "I've been working on it since we arrived," he answered. "It's a hand!"

Fascinated, the man from the north examined the simple device. It was a crudely shaped fist that had been pounded out of iron. It was attached to a metal brace and leather straps fitted with buckles. "Well, I will be," he said. He then held it up to his right arm and asked, "How does it work?"

Son helped him fasten the fist to the end of his arm. Though it was unnatural-looking, it still looked less jarring than the empty space that was there before. "Now you can punch through anything!" the boy declared.

"I believe I can," Dulnear agreed with an amused grin. His heart beat faster as he held the fist aloft, and he turned his arm over so he could see it from all angles. Something about the metallic contraption returned a small feeling of normality to the man. "I do not know what to say. Thank you, Son."

"You're welcome," the boy said. "I was happy to make it for you. Aesef helped me with the bracing."

"But it was Son's idea," the farmer added. "He wanted to surprise you."

"Indeed I am surprised," the man from the north said, and he wrapped his arms around his young friend. "A thousand times, thank you!"

When he was done hugging, the boy announced excitedly, "I'm going to go get Maren so I can show her!" and he ran out of the room.

Dulnear adjusted one of the leather straps on the makeshift prosthetic. There was nothing between the straps and his forearm, and he noticed that they were leaving an impression. He was so taken aback by the boy's gesture that he lost himself staring at the device. "If only it held a sword," he mused.

"Now you know what he's been doing out in the barn all this time," Aesef said.

The man from the north broke from his fixation on the hand and looked at the old man. Still smiling, he expressed, "Thank you for helping him. I do not know how I could repay you for all you have done for me."

"You already have," the farmer said with a smile. He then took a deep breath and added, "But I have to be honest. I don't think a metal fist will be enough to defend yourself from Thorndel or his kin."

Dulnear knew that his friend was right. "I know it is a fool's errand," he explained. "But I have to try."

"And what if you should run into Thorndel on your journey?" Aesef asked. "The children have already lost you once. It would ruin them to lose you again."

Dulnear looked away and pondered the farmer's words. "I do not know, it is just that…" As he trailed off, his head became dizzy, and it felt as if the room was spinning. He wanted to continue, but saying another word felt like lifting a weight that he didn't have the strength to bear.

Aesef's voice broke through. "You care for her deeply, don't you?" he asked.

The man from the north nodded his head yes. "Very much," he said, bringing his attention back to the iron hand.

"How do you think she would feel about you returning to Tuas-arum?"

"I am sure she would insist that I did not," he answered honestly.

"And there's no way I could talk you out of it?" Aesef asked.

"None at all."

Before the farmer could make another plea, Son and Maren came bounding into the room. They stopped in front of Dulnear and the boy shouted, "See, I told you I made him a hand!"

Maren stood there holding a large book in her left hand, and with her right hand she was massaging her ear. She smiled big and began to whisper to herself, "Fist. Smash. Pshhhh. Ahhh."

Dulnear leaned toward the girl, holding out his arm. "Would you like to get a better look?" he asked.

"Yes," she said as she took her hand off of her ear so she could feel the hunk of iron and the attached bracing that held it in place. "Are you going to smash the table?" she asked with eyebrows raised.

"No, but later on we can find some things to smash outside. How does that sound?" the man asked.

An unsuccessfully suppressed smile crept across Maren's face. She made a fist and lightly touched it to the metal one. "Yessssss," she said softly, and then ran out of the room.

Son looked like he was about to follow her out until Dulnear grabbed his attention. "Son, can you stay moment? I need to talk to you about my trip north."

The boy sighed as he turned back toward the man. "Do you really have to go?"

The man from the north looked at Son's disappointed face and searched for the right words to say. "I am afraid I do," he began. "But this time, the plan is to return."

"To Laor?" the boy asked.

"Yes, to Laor. I only have to retrieve something from

my estate, and then I will never return to the north again," Dulnear said, keeping eye contact with the boy.

"How long will you be gone?" Son asked.

"Gone where?" a voice asked from the doorway. Faymia was standing there. Maren was standing next to her, pointing at the new hand attached to Dulnear's arm.

Son's eyes widened and the color ran out of his cheeks. He moved closer to Dulnear's ear and whispered, "You haven't told her?"

"Gone where?" the woman asked again.

The man from the north stood and faced Faymia. He knew he was going to have to share his plans with her eventually, but was tentative about the conversation nonetheless. Swallowing, he explained, "I have to go back to Tuas-arum."

A look of dismay covered the woman's face. "But why?" she asked.

"There is something I need there. It is something that will keep Tcharron, and his slavers, away from you forever," he said.

Faymia took a small step back. Her lip quivered as she spoke, "I can't believe this." She shook her head and continued, "I can't allow you to risk your life again on account of me."

"I know it sounds foolish," the man admitted, "but I must."

The woman stood tall and pressed her shoulders back. "Well, if you're going back on account of me, then I'm going with you!" she exclaimed.

Everything in Dulnear wanted to protest, but he did not. He would have died if not for her company on their previous journey, and she would be no better off if he died on this one. He licked his lips and said solemnly, "So be it."

Suddenly, Son chimed in, "And I'm going too!"

"I'm sorry, it is too perilous, Son." Dulnear said.

"I've been training for a long time," the boy objected. "Besides, you said that you're no match for Thorndel left-handed."

"'Tis true, but you are no match for him with either hand."

"Maybe so, but I'm sure the three of us can find a way to beat him—if we run into him, that is," the boy said optimistically.

Dulnear looked at Faymia, and then back at Son. He knew the boy would follow, even if he was told not to. "Okay, but we have a lot of preparation to do in a very short time. And what of Maren?"

"I'll keep her here," Aesef offered. "I'm sure she'll enjoy reading and playing with Phel."

"Thank you," Dulnear said. "Now, I suppose I will need to practice my left-handed swordsmanship."

"And smashing stuff!" Maren added.

"And smashing stuff," the man from the north replied.

Several days later, Dulnear and Son were practicing swordplay in one of the fallow fields on Aesef's farm. The man from the north was impressed by how much the boy had grown in his fighting skills. "You are doing very well!" he complimented. "I am glad we are on the same side."

"Thank you! I learned from the best," Son said as he

blocked a downward strike and countered with a lunge. "Are you sure you're not left-handed?" he asked with a grin. "I can hardly keep up with you."

Dulnear returned the smile and moved out of the way of the boy's attack with a speed that seemed unnatural for a man of his size. The swordplay, and the boy's company, seemed to fill him with a greater sense of strength and vigor. At times during their training, he even laughed as they exchanged strikes and parries.

Before long, Dulnear noticed that they had an audience. Faymia and Maren were standing nearby. The young girl had a branch in her hand, mimicking their moves and slashing through the air with surprisingly good form and speed.

"She wanted to come watch you practice," Faymia explained.

"I see," the man from the north said. He then looked at Maren, knelt on one knee, and encouraged her, "Your technique is nearly perfect. I hope that you never need to use it."

"Me too!" the girl said as she whacked the large man's forearm with the branch.

Dulnear rubbed his arm and let out a playful, "Youch! Are you trying to remove the rest of my arm?"

"Uh huh," she said with a giggle. Then, looking away, she expressed in a whisper, "Pshhh. Ahhhh! I got you!"

The man from the north chuckled and gave the girl a wink. Suddenly, an idea came to him like a splash of cold water to the face. He stood up and spun around to speak to the boy. "Son, can you alter the iron fist you gave me to include a gauntlet that reaches to here?" he said as he pointed to just below his right elbow.

His young friend wore a curious expression for a moment, then a smile crept over his face. "You want to use your arm as a shield, don't you."

Dulnear beamed, "You got it, lad. Can it be done?"

"I have plenty of iron," the boy said. "And I'm sure Aesef can assist me. Is it okay if it takes a couple of days?"

"Of course it is," the man from the north said as he pushed up his coat sleeve, removed the metal hand, and handed it to the boy.

Son held the device in his arms and examined the place where the fist attached to the bracing. "I'll get started right now. Maren can help!" he exclaimed as he started to run toward the barn.

As the young girl ran after him, she could be heard asking, "Can we smash things with it?"

"We'll see!" the boy shouted back, and they disappeared into the distance.

Dulnear and Faymia now stood alone in the field. It was the first time they had been alone together since he first began to recover. For a moment, he lost himself looking at the woman's face. Her silver eyes were powerful under the textured gray sky. Her hair was braided, but the loose hairs whipped over her forehead as the wind blew them about. "I can see why you love them," she said, breaking his transfixion.

Hoping the woman didn't notice that he was staring, he said fondly, "Yes, they are my treasure."

Faymia smiled and let out a quiet chuckle.

"What is so funny?" Dulnear asked, smiling with her.

"You seem different when you're with the children," she explained. "It's a side of you that I never expected to see."

"You do not like it?" he asked.

"I like it very much," she said. She paused as if she were trying to think of the right words to say. "It's your eyes. When Son and Maren are near, your eyes look like they have the sun behind them, and they show no trace of all of the things you've been through."

Dulnear thought about her words and it dawned on him how true they were. He felt strong and full of purpose around the children. "When I met the boy, I taught him the ways of a warrior. He was so uncertain and alone, like a lost pup. As we became friends, he taught me how to be patient and gentle," he said. "He is like my own."

Faymia looked away for a moment, then asked, "Are you sure it's a good idea to bring him to Tuas-arum? Is it a good idea for any of us to go?"

"I am not sure of anything," the man from the north said honestly. He allowed the woman's question to settle in. "I am only sure of my purpose for going. I believe it agrees with the heart of the Great Father."

There was pain in Faymia's eyes and her forehead wrinkled slightly. "But isn't that what you believed before you lost your hand?" she asked.

Dulnear looked down and gathered his thoughts. He wasn't used to having his decisions questioned, but he knew there was truth in what his friend was implying. He glanced at the sky, then at the woman, and said, "I suppose I am learning that being on the side of right is not a guarantee of success." He rubbed his chin and continued, "But I cannot abandon what is right for the sake of safety or comfort."

"But if you acted in alignment with the heart of the Great Father, then why didn't he protect you?" the woman pressed as a tear formed in her eye.

Faymia's last question seemed to sink deep into his chest. For a moment, he could hear nothing but his own breathing as his mind searched for answers. "The Great Father is good," he began. "In fact, there is nothing in him that is not good. Water is wet, fire is hot, ice is cold, and he is good. It is his nature to be so. I am a flawed man, and if I have a standard of goodness that is different from his, then it is I who am wrong, not he. I am learning this as I ponder what has happened."

"But it's not fair," the woman argued before looking away.

"No, it is not," Dulnear agreed. "But fairness and goodness are not the same. Goodness is much greater, but sometimes harder to see. And though I do not fully see the goodness in losing my hand, I am learning to trust that one day I will."

Faymia moved closer to the man from the north. With a tear falling down her cheek, she rested her head on his chest. "It's just that," she began, "the children aren't the only ones who couldn't bear to lose you again."

Dulnear wrapped his arms around his friend and tried to comfort her. Many words came to him but they all seemed trite, and flat, and he felt that she deserved better. She wept for a while and when she was finished, she looked into his eyes. As she did, something stirred in him, and he felt that he finally understood her thoughts.

"I promise that I will do everything to protect not just you and the boy, but myself as well," he said.

"Promise?" she asked with a glimmer of hope on her face.

"Yes, I have made my restitution, even if Thorndel chooses not to acknowledge it," he said. "I am not going to surrender my life, but to claim something from my own home. I do not envy the man who tries to get in our way."

Dulnear was admiring the handiwork of Son and Aesef. He had the new fist buckled around his arm, and it now included an iron sleeve that went almost to his elbow. "My, this is nice," he said as he turned his arm over. "It should stop any blade."

"I'm glad you like it," Son said. "Aesef helped lots, especially with the hammering."

The old farmer added modestly, "But it was mostly Son."

"Well, I am impressed with both of you," the man from the north said.

The five of them stood outside of the house. They had all eaten a hearty breakfast and Dulnear, Faymia, and Son were prepared to leave for Tuas-arum.

"Thank you again," the man from the north expressed to Aesef.

The farmer raised his eyebrows and asked, "Are you sure I can't persuade you to stay?"

"I am sure," Dulnear answered. "But we will not be gone long. I have this little one to return for." He gestured toward Maren, who was standing next to Faymia with her head resting against the woman's side.

Aesef smiled and said, "The girl has become quite taken with her. Make sure you bring her back safely."

"I will fight to the death to defend her," the northerner declared.

"Well, let's hope it doesn't come to that," the farmer murmured.

"I'll fight too!" Son added.

Just then, Aesef's servant, Phel, came upon the circle of friends. He was leading two horses by their reins. "Ah, here they are," the farmer exclaimed. "I want you to take these horses. For you, my friend, the largest in the stable, and another powerful steed for Son and Faymia to share."

Dulnear was amazed by the act of generosity. "I cannot take your horses. You have already done so much."

"I insist," Aesef replied. "If you run into trouble, it will be much easier to outrun it. Besides, this way, you will be able to return much sooner."

"I do not know what to say," the man from the north said. "Thank you, my friend."

"You're welcome," the farmer said as he walked over to the larger of the two horses. "This is Mor. She's strong and loyal."

Dulnear walked over to the animal and cheerfully introduced himself. "Very nice to meet you, Mor," he said as he gently stroked the side of its neck and blew a deep breath toward its nostrils. The horse sniffed the air and gave a relaxed sigh as her new rider continued to pet her.

Aesef then walked over to the other horse and introduced him. "And this is Tapp, my fastest horse."

Son awkwardly approached the animal and attempted to imitate Dulnear's actions. Tapp gave a restless stomp until Faymia joined the boy and scratched behind the horse's ears. It gave the woman a smell and immediately calmed down.

"I have my mule!" Maren chimed in. "His name is Earl!"

"Of course you do," Aesef said to the girl. "Later, will you show me how you ride him?"

"Uh huh!" she said with a grin.

There was a quiet pause as the group looked at each other. Dulnear wished he could stop time to make the moment last a little longer, but he knew that, for Faymia's sake, they had to leave. It had already been weeks since he'd arrived at his friend's farm, and he couldn't hide the woman there forever. He took a deep breath and said, "We must be going, but I promise to be as swift as possible." He then lifted Maren up and squeezed her as she hugged his neck. "I will miss you. Be good," he said before setting her back down.

The little girl said, "Goodbye!" as she ran back to Faymia for a last hug, then said her goodbyes to Son.

When all of their farewells were said, the travelers mounted their horses. Son sat in front of Faymia, atop Tapp. He had no previous experience riding a horse, so she coached him in the proper way to hold the reins and steer the animal.

They made their way across the northern fields, discussing their expectations for the amount of time their trip would take, how they would camp, and other details. But as the road drew nearer, Dulnear felt a growing tightness in his chest. He prayed for an uneventful journey, but a lingering unease whispered in his ear, and he found it difficult to be at peace.

CHAPTER FOURTEEN
ALL THAT CAN BURN

T HE TRAVELERS MADE THEIR WAY swiftly to the northern border, moving through towns and villages without stopping, and doing their best to avoid the attention of other travelers. When they reached the Contuent Bridge, Dulnear slowed his horse to take in the sight of the Fuar River below. The mist of the rushing water touched his face, and the memory of his last passing of the river seemed like a dream that weighed on him with a strange melancholy.

Son rode Tapp up next to the man and asked, "Are we getting closer?"

"This is the river that divides the north and south of Aun," Dulnear explained. "At the speed we have been traveling, we should be at my estate by tomorrow evening." He then glanced at Faymia and let his eyes linger on her lovely face for a moment. She showed great patience and care as she taught Son to ride their horse, and it drew his heart nearer to hers. As a result, he felt an even greater passion for his final mission to Tuas-arum. "It seems as if we were just here," he said to her.

The woman wore a thoughtful expression. "The last

time we were here, you were almost too sick to walk. I thought I was going to have to put you over my shoulder and carry you across the bridge," she joked.

"I believe you could," the man from the north laughed, and they continued on.

As the day faded, they found a place to camp. It was far off the road, and well hidden by a circle of tall rocks and trees. They fed and watered the horses, then made a fire to cook rabbits that Faymia had hunted with her bow and arrows.

"This is a delicious dinner," Son said to Faymia as he took another bite of his rabbit.

"Thank you," she said, adding, "Dulnear gave me this beautiful bow to catch them with."

The boy opened up his gray coat and withdrew a brightly polished sword with northern runes adorning the pommel. "This is Onaire," he exclaimed. "He gave me this just before our battle at the ravine." He smiled proudly, then put the weapon away.

Faymia looked across the fire at Dulnear. "He's a great man," she said, smiling.

Warmed by their compliments, yet embarrassed by the attention, the man from the north shifted the conversation. "When I met the boy, he ate only turnips."

"Very funny!" Son retorted. "I just didn't know how to hunt yet. I didn't even like turnips."

"You hunted turnips like a professional," Dulnear jabbed, then laughed as he reached over and rubbed the boy's shoulder. "I am very proud to see how far you've come, lad," he said. Then he added, "I think it would be good if we got some rest though. Tomorrow will probably be a very long day for all of us."

The following evening, the trio approached Dulnear's estate along the winding northerly road. The veiled sun was fading, but there was still enough gray light to see for a great distance. When they were upon his property, the man halted his horse until Faymia and Son were next to him.

"Son," the man whispered. "Come over to my horse. I want to show you something." He lifted the boy from his horse and set him on Mor so he could whisper in his ear from behind him. He then leaned toward Faymia and said quietly, "Ride beside us. I want to show him the estate."

Hearing his friend's words, the boy perked up and asked, "Where is your land?"

Urging his horse forward, Dulnear answered, "Look to the east. It is mine, almost as far as you can see."

The boy's mouth was agape as they slowly rode the path in front of the property. With eyes wide, he took in the rolling fields and enormous oak trees. "This is incredible," he said with enthusiasm while trying to remain quiet.

"This is where I learned to fight, to read, to hunt, and to farm," the man explained. "Do you remember when I told you about tricking my brother into jumping into a pile of leaves?"

"Yes, that was hilarious!" Son bubbled.

"Well, way back there is the tree," Dulnear indicated.

Faymia sat up with an amused smile. "So that is why

you were giggling as we ran for our lives? You duped your little brother into leaping into dead leaves?" she asked.

"Yes," the man grinned. "I was in very much trouble from my father for it."

"Your father sounds wise," the woman chuckled.

The man from the north then pointed to the large house in the distance and said to the boy, "And that is my house."

"It's immense!" Son exclaimed as his eyebrows raised higher.

"I never ran out of hiding spaces," the man from the north joked. "My brother and I could play hide-and-seek for days!"

"Did you have your own room?" the boy asked.

"Of course," the warrior answered. "The house has been in my clan for generations. My great-great-great-grandfather, who had many children, built it. But my father only had two sons, so there was more than enough room for us."

Son continued to stare at the massive house. Under his breath, he murmured, "Wow!"

When the mansion came closer into view, Dulnear noticed a light flickering in one of the windows. He grew agitated and growled, "That greedy dog Thorndel is squatting in my home again. He's too lazy to track me, and too rapacious to let my estate rest."

"What are we going to do?" the boy asked.

The man from the north breathed deeply through flared nostrils, clenched his jaw, and answered, "Burn it all."

"What?!" Son asked with surprise. "This is your home, and it's the most magnificent one I've ever seen."

"I know, boy, but I mean never to return here," Dulnear explained. "And I can't bear to think of others coming to dishonor my family. Thorndel has already defaced my father's portrait, and who knows what else. Let us head back in the direction we came. We will need to tie up the horses and discuss our actions."

"Are you sure you want to do that?" Faymia asked.

"He has a thing for fire," Son joked.

Dulnear didn't think it was funny. He merely raised an eyebrow toward the boy, then answered the woman's question. "I am sure," he answered. He thought about his life in the north, the people and events that held influence over him for many years, and the person he had become since leaving. He continued, "There is nothing for me in the north anymore, and having a mansion here only ties my heart to a place of violence, pain, and loss. I feel a weight lifted from my shoulders just thinking of burning it all down."

The woman looked away and bit her lip. Squeezing her hands into tightly rolled fists, she looked back at Dulnear and asked, "What do you want me to do?"

"First, it is important that Thorndel does not see either of you before you enter the house," the man began. "In the outbuilding, where the cart was stored, there are several jars of oil. I will draw the louse outside. When he comes, you and Son go into the house with the oil, spread it, light it, and run back to the horses as quickly as you can."

"What about you?" the boy asked.

"I will confront the son of Shenndel," Dulnear answered.

"But I thought you were no match for him left-handed," Son pressed, with a growing expression of concern.

The man from the north looked toward his house and mustered his courage. Inhaling deeply, he claimed, "I am much better than I was. Besides, he will not be expecting the iron fist."

The boy did not appear to be comforted, nor did Faymia. "You promised to be careful," the woman said. "You don't have to do this on my account."

The warrior looked into her eyes. "This is just as much for me as it is for you," he said. "And I do promise to be vigilant."

The boy and the runaway slave embraced Dulnear tightly. "Please be alive when we come back," she said.

"I promise," the man answered. "Now go. I have a squatter to evict."

"Thorndel, son of Shenndel!" Dulnear shouted. He stood several steps away from the large front door to the house, looking up to the second-story window where the light flickered. "Thorndel, come and fight me!" he jeered. "Prove that you are more than a lazy guttersnipe!"

A large silhouetted figure appeared in the window, then disappeared quickly. The man from the north stepped back a few paces, then took several deep breaths as he waited for his opponent. Suddenly, the door swung open, and there stood Thorndel with sword drawn. His curly, black hair and beard looked more disheveled than usual, and his fur reeked of whisky.

"There you are!" Dulnear exclaimed. "I was expecting you to come and find me, but you have been here all along."

"I was just making my plan," Thorndel said indignantly.

"I bet you were," Dulnear said with a sarcastic grin. "And I am sure your plan involved stinking up my house while you came up with cowardly excuses not to pursue me."

"Those are brave words for a Nairetu!" his enemy retorted arrogantly. "Why would you be so foolish as to come here?"

"I knew my hand was not enough for you," he explained, "and I am not fond of surprises, so I thought I would come and end this so I can finally get some peace."

"Get some peace?!" Thorndel shouted. "Killing me would only rekindle the wrath of my father. He would gather his friends and slay you without pity."

"Ha!" Dulnear laughed. "He would be too ashamed that his son was defeated by a one-handed man. He would probably stay home and cry in his bed!"

"You simple fool!" the embittered warrior cried. "Whether I vanquish you, or you slay me, the happy ending you seek is not possible."

"Then I accept your surrender," the man from the north crowed. "You may lay down your sword." He intended to rile the man, clouding his judgement and dulling his skills.

"And why in all of Aun would I surrender to you, Marhail?" Thorndel asked with a look of disgust.

"You tell me," Dulnear taunted. "You seem certain that I would kill you, and that your father would avenge your death. In addition, your father would need help from his friends to do it. I am only trying to spare you by allowing you to cede."

Thorndel wrinkled his forehead and hesitated for a moment before saying, "I did not say my father would need help."

"Then why would he gather his friends?" the man from the north asked.

"Just because!" the exasperated squatter answered. He then inhaled deeply, clenched his teeth together and snarled, "You killed my brother, and I will not rest until I see your eyes glazed over with death and your blood soaking the ground."

"You cannot win, Thorndel," Dulnear said confidently. "There would be no glory in defeating a Nairetu, and being defeated by one would bring enormous shame. Why do you not just go home and let it go?"

The rancorous northerner looked off to the distance. "Because I cannot," he stated.

"Then indeed I am sorry," the iron-fisted warrior said.

Thorndel's eyes snapped back to his opponent's. "Sorry? For what?"

"I did not want to battle your brother, but he insisted. I offered myself in restitution and your father took my hand, but it was not enough for you. You insist on the way of destruction, even when you have the freedom to walk away from it, so you force my hand to slay you." Dulnear then reached into his long fur coat, withdrew his father's sword, and continued, "And I will kill your father, your cousin, and any of your other family members who choose to pursue me. I will leave a trail of blood across Northern Aun like none has ever seen before, and when it is over, you will be remembered as Thorndel the stupid, who would not walk away, and could not defeat a one-handed man."

Thorndel's hands shook. Beads of sweat were forming on his forehead and his eyes squinted. He glanced at Dulnear's right arm, then looked into his eyes before raising his sword to attack.

Dulnear blocked Thorndel's blade as if he could read the man's mind. He could feel his confidence rise as they battled, and he fought left-handed with the skill of one who had been doing it his entire life. "Concede!" he demanded. "You cannot win!"

Breathing heavily, his enemy responded, "I have grown quite accustomed to your estate, and I have no intention of leaving now." He then lunged forward in an attempt to sink his sword into Dulnear's chest.

Dulnear blocked the sword downward, but Thorndel used the momentum from the block to swing his sword upward and struck him on the right shoulder. Dulnear grimaced from the pain, and the wound immediately began to throb and bleed. If not for the heavy fur coat, the cut would have been much deeper. He used his sword's pommel to force his opponent's blade backward, almost taking off his ear.

They each took a step back from the other. Thorndel reached up to touch his ear, and Dulnear shrugged his shoulder to assess the damage. Circling each other, the man from the north said, "Well, I am afraid there will not be much of an estate left after tonight. My friends are inside now, preparing to burn it to the ground."

The sides of Thorndel's mouth curled in a sinister grin.

He then laughed, "Your friends are dead then. Searfain is inside, and he enjoys killing southerners. Others are coming too. You and your pathetic companions came here to die."

Son followed Faymia through the rear entrance to the house. They each carried a large pot of oil down the narrow corridor, past the library. Quietly, the boy asked, "Where should we start spreading this?"

"Just follow me," she said, and headed down the hallway to the foyer, then up the grand staircase.

The boy was astounded by the magnificence of the mansion. Even though it was getting dark, and difficult to see, he felt that he was in a place of greatness, and it caused him to think of his rugged friend in a new way.

They passed the second floor and ascended to the third. It was covered with dust and cobwebs, and looked as if it hadn't been visited for many years. Son tiptoed to the end of the hallway and opened one of the doors. There, he found a room with a child's bed, and many wooden toys strewn about. He wondered if they were Dulnear's, and thought about what it must have been like to grow up with so much.

"Let's start here," the woman said, and she carefully began pouring oil along the walls. "Don't use too much," she added. "The greatest amount should go on the first floor."

Son nodded and began distributing some of his oil. It was difficult to keep it from spilling onto himself since the jar was so full, and the fuel sloshed about. The smell of it reminded him of the confrontation at the ravine on Aesef's farm, and he had to remind himself to remain in the moment. They spread some throughout most of the third-floor rooms but endeavored to move quickly for the sake of their friend.

When they were satisfied, they descended to the second floor to do the same. They began at the end of the hallway that was opposite from the drawing room, the room where the flickering lantern light emanated from.

Eventually, they reached the room that once belonged to Dulnear's father. Son marveled at the weapons mounted on the walls, and Faymia showed him where Dulnear had provided her with a bow and sword. It was painful for the boy to pour oil in this room. It didn't feel right to destroy a place that held such importance to his friend, even if his friend was asking him to do it. "Should we really be doing this?" he asked in a whisper. "It just seems wrong."

The runaway slave paused for a moment, and answered quietly, "I can't believe that we're doing this either. But one thing I know is that Dulnear has risked his life to save mine more than once. I owe him my trust."

Son remembered the times his large friend rescued him, and said simply, "Me too." They then exited the room and continued down the hallway. Suddenly, they were halted by the sight of a large man standing on the opposite side of the staircase.

The man stood silently for a moment, staring at the two with a puzzled expression. He then withdrew a large sword from his belt and demanded, "Who are you?"

Son knew there was no answer he could give that would cause the man to put his sword away. He immediately set his pot of oil down at the top of the stairs and took out his sword. "Get out of here!" he shouted to Faymia as he charged the northerner.

The man sliced through the air with his sword but missed as Son slid along the floor, through the brute's legs. The boy thrust his blade into the back of the man's thigh, then immediately rolled out of the way.

The large man released a guttural cry of pain as his left leg buckled beneath him, bringing him down closer to Son's height. As he pushed on his knee with his left hand in an attempt to stand up again, he swiped toward the boy with the sword in his right hand, almost catching Son's neck.

The lad lunged at the man but was knocked back when the barbarian landed a backhand with his returning fist. The boy laid dazed as he watched the man return to his feet, cursing the pain in his bleeding leg. The northerner raised his sword over his head to strike the boy but froze when an arrow sank into his ribcage. Faymia stood a few feet away, releasing arrow after arrow into the man, but it hardly seemed to slow him down.

Son scrambled to his feet and swiped at the man's left hand, nearly taking off a finger. Howling with rage, the northerner tucked the bleeding hand under his right arm and began swinging his sword wildly. The boy ducked and dodged the enormous sword but was unable to make another attack.

Faymia slung her bow over her shoulder and withdrew her sword. While the northerner was occupied with Son, she managed to stab him in the side. The large man growled, then pulled one of the arrows from his body and begun swinging it at Son with his injured left hand while he attacked the woman with the sword in his right hand.

The man swiped the arrow toward Son's head but the boy met his large hand with his blade. The man was stunned for a moment and Son took advantage of it. He swung hard and removed the man's fore and middle fingers. In a sudden, erratic motion, the man jerked his right hand upward, causing the tip of his sword to catch Faymia's left eye. She screamed and dropped her sword as she reached for her face in pain. Son then plunged his sword into the man's left leg again in a rapid stabbing motion before spinning to the other side of him, retrieving the woman's sword and pulling her toward the staircase.

The northerner dropped to his hands and knees, spewing savage threats at the two. Son grabbed Faymia's pot of oil with one arm and used his other arm to help escort the bleeding woman away. When he saw his own oil pot sitting at the top of the stairs he kicked it over, causing the slippery liquid to spill down the staircase.

Avoiding the spilled oil, they reached the first floor. When they did, Son looked at Faymia. She was covering her injured eye with one hand but keeping her other eye on their surroundings. "Take me back down the hallway we entered the house through," she instructed. "In the library, there is a tinderbox filled with matches."

They swiftly reached the library, and Faymia showed Son where the matches were kept. "Over there, by the window," she explained. It was almost pitch-dark in the room, and the boy fumbled his way over to the matches.

"Got 'em!" he announced, and they went back out into the narrow hall.

"Great! Let's light the oil and get out," the woman said, still holding her hand over her eye.

As they moved back toward the foyer, the boy pocketed the matches and said, "Wait here while I finish this." Before the woman had a chance to protest, he ran back out into the foyer to pour out the rest of the oil.

While in the foyer, Son could hear the clashing of swords outside. He knew it was Dulnear and Thorndel, and his heart pounded as he considered the outcome of their battle. Suddenly, he heard a booming voice yell, "I'll kill you!" and he looked to see the wounded northerner standing at the top of the stairs.

Son threw the oil pot as far as he could, and he could hear it shatter in the distance. He then took out his sword and stood in a ready stance. "Come down here so I can take the rest of your hand!" he shouted to the raging goon.

The northerner stepped onto the staircase, his wounded leg slowing him down. He took one step, and then another. He then stepped directly into the oil that Son had allowed to spill on the stairs. He slipped and tumbled down the stairs like a giant rag doll.

When the man reached the bottom of the stairs Son ran over to him, ready to strike before the man could recover. The man's eyes were wide open and his neck was bent in a strange way. Son realized that he was dead, so he put his sword away and headed back to the narrow hallway.

When the boy was at the edge of the foyer, he took a match from the tinderbox, lit it, and tossed it into the middle of the room. It landed in the oil and the fire spread quickly, illuminating the grand mansion with monstrous orange flames. Son watched for a moment as the greatest home he had ever seen was engulfed in a blaze.

Dulnear's heart pounded like a blacksmith's hammer. He clenched his teeth and gripped his sword tightly. The two had been circling for several minutes, trading words, and only clashing occasionally. The man tried hard to focus, believing that his friends were skilled and resourceful enough to get out of the house alive. He took a deep breath, whispered a silent prayer, then swiped his sword toward Thorndel's neck.

His enemy blocked the attack and the two of them erupted in a flurry of steel, muscle, and sweat. Like two spinning tops brawling they dueled, knowing that only one of them would survive the night.

Dulnear now bled freely from the wound on his shoulder. He tried to push the pain out of his mind, along with the nagging fear for the safety of his friends. He began to regret coming back to the north, and was terrified that his desire to help Faymia might have killed her and Son. He struck downward toward Thorndel's head but the agitator blocked, locking the sword with his hilt. Thorndel now had control and was forcing the blade toward Dulnear's neck.

As the two grappled, Thorndel taunted, "You are an absurd failure. I now have the pleasure of watching you get what you deserve for the second time."

Dulnear knew he would lose the grapple with only his left hand. He curled his lip and executed an iron-fisted roundhouse punch to Thorndel's temple, causing him to stumble backward. With an injured shoulder, the punch caused Dulnear immense discomfort, but he showed no sign of pain.

Thorndel shook his head and focused his eyes on Dulnear. He began to ask, "What have you got there, some kind of—"

Dulnear cut him off with another punch to the face, this time breaking his opponent's nose.

Stunned, the vengeful brute shouted, "You broke my—"

But again Dulnear swung, landing a metal fist to the mouth, knocking loose a front tooth.

The embittered northerner wiped the blood from his face and howled in rage as he began to swing his blade wildly.

Using both his sword and the iron prosthetic, Dulnear blocked each blow, but Thorndel's savage aggression kept him on the defense.

Thorndel managed to land another strike to Dulnear's shoulder. The pain raced up his neck and down his arm, rendering the iron fist useless. The man from the north was forced back against the house, desperately attempting to keep his enemy's broadsword from cutting him again. Suddenly, Thorndel's eyes grew wide. He stepped back and cried, "No!"

Dulnear could smell smoke, and saw flames through the corner of his eye. A renewed strength came over him and he lunged at Thorndel, piercing his ribcage, and giving the sword a quick twist before removing it. Willing his left arm to remain strong and swift, he fought like a drowning man fights to reach the surface of the water. His opponent was now on the defense, holding his weapon with one hand, and stopping the flow of blood from his abdomen with the other.

As the fire grew, so did the warrior's ability to see his surroundings. At the very edge of visibility, Dulnear could see another northerner fast approaching from the direction of the road. Dulnear was weary and bloodied, but determined to fight until his heart ceased to beat. He continued to advance against Thorndel until he landed a devastating blow against his already broken nose with the pommel of his sword.

Thorndel stumbled backward, staggering under pain and blood loss. "I cannot believe you would burn it," he exclaimed. "You had everything a man could want!"

Dulnear paused and said, "My father was unable to take any of it with him when he died, as was his father, and those before him. The greatest treasures I have, I found when I walked away from this estate. I should have burned it a long time ago." He then glanced over his enemy's shoulder to see that the approaching northerner was closer now.

Noticing the glance, Thorndel looked behind him, then back toward Dulnear. He began to laugh, "I told you others were coming! Tonight, the great Dulnear dies." He then brought his sword down toward Dulnear's wounded shoulder.

Dulnear immediately blocked the strike, then counterattacked, slicing Thorndel's chest just below his collarbone in the process, sending the man another step backward, grasping at the fresh wound. He brought his sword down hard, disarming him. Dulnear growled and kicked the man square in the chest, sending him to the ground.

"Wait!" Thorndel pleaded, lying on his back. "Please don't kill me!"

Dulnear noticed that the approaching figure now had his sword drawn and was racing toward them. "Not to worry, wastrel, I will be sending you company soon," he said as he raised his sword over his head to strike the final blow.

"Stop!" the approaching man shouted. "Do not do it!"

As the man stepped into full view behind the fallen northerner, Dulnear could see that it was Brunnlyn. Thorndel's cousin looked intently at the bleeding, one-handed swordsman, and he stood in a fierce fighting stance.

From the ground, Thorndel began to taunt, "What now, Marhail? What now? My cousin is here to kill you. Perhaps we will cut off your other hand and display it on the mantel."

Brunnlyn stood over the taunting man and looked down at him with a pained expression. He sighed and quietly said, "I am sorry, cousin. Please forgive me." He then plunged his sword through the heart of the wrathful Thorndel, silencing him forever.

Dulnear couldn't believe what he had just seen. He took a small step back and blinked. "Why did you do that?" he gasped.

Brunnlyn pulled his sword from Thorndel's chest, wiped the blade on the grass, then placed it back in his belt. He looked at his palms for a moment, then explained, "You would never know the peace you seek if you had killed him. Now retribution will fall on me, and you are free to live your life in the south."

Dulnear was stunned by his answer. He shook his head as he gazed into the night sky. "Why would you do that for me?" he asked.

"You have shown me that there is a better way than hatred and violence, and you were willing to die for that better way," Brunnlyn answered. "Besides, you have already sacrificed so much, and it is not right for Thorndel to demand more."

Still astonished by what he had just seen and heard, Dulnear put his sword away, and asked, "What will you do?"

"I will take my cousin's body to my uncle," he said. He then looked down and continued, "My fate will be in his hands."

"Why do you not run?" Dulnear asked. "You do not have to subject yourself to that bitter old man."

"I cannot. There must be no mistake about who killed Thorndel or you risk another confrontation," Brunnlyn answered.

"I do not know what to say," the man from the north uttered. "Thank you. I owe you my life."

"Then live it well," Brunnlyn said. "And I will try to do the same." He then hefted his cousin's lifeless body over his shoulders and began walking back toward the road.

Dulnear watched the man walk off, thinking deeply about what had just happened. Then, shaking him from his thoughts, Son appeared before him. "Dulnear! Faymia is hurt!" he yelled, and the two of them ran back to their horses.

Dulnear, Son, and Faymia stood with the horses as close to the burning mansion as they could without the heat being overwhelming. It was the only way the man from the north could see well enough to attend to his friend's wound. He had Son retrieve some pine sap and he used it to close the cut under Faymia's eye.

"This resin has been quite indispensable lately," the one-handed warrior said as he carefully applied it to the wound.

The woman trembled as her friend attended to her. "I can't see out of that eye," she said.

Dulnear carefully looked into the blood-red, damaged eye. He knew that she would never see from it again but hesitated to tell her. Finally he said, "I am afraid that eye has seen its last." He then held her close as she wept into his chest. "I am so sorry," he said. "I believed that anyone inside would have come outside to face me. I did not know that Searfain would be waiting for you."

When Faymia had finished crying, she sat down in the grass to rest. Son fashioned a sling for Dulnear's arm and tended to the wounds on his shoulder. He then stored the heavy iron fist with his other belongings on the massive Mor. "What do we do now?" he asked his friend.

Dulnear sat down next to Faymia and gazed at the burning house. He felt sorrow, relief, and anticipation, all at the same time. Memories played through his mind as he saw flames burst through windows and heard the crashing of timber inside. "Now, I suppose we watch it burn," he said.

The three of them sat on the ground together, occasionally wincing when a loud crash could be heard, or commenting on the floating sparks that danced above the house. Eventually Son and Faymia fell asleep, leaning against their large friend. But Dulnear stayed awake, watching all that represented his old life blaze through the night.

CHAPTER FIFTEEN
The Ransom

THE NEXT MORNING, DULNEAR SAT near a small fire drinking a cup of coffee and reading from an old, leather-bound book. His house was now a blackened stone shell that contained the broken, smoldering wreckage of the night before.

When Son awoke, he rubbed his eyes, glanced at the burned mansion, then at Dulnear and asked, "Is it time to get going?"

The man from the north took a last swig of coffee, closed his book, and stood. "Good morning," he said. "Yes, it is almost time." He then walked over to Faymia, who was still sleeping in the grass. He looked at her face, which had now turned a plumb and yellow color around her left cheek and eye. "We just need to take care of a couple things first. By any chance, was there a wagon in the shed when you went to fetch the oil?" he asked.

Son thought for a moment, then answered, "Yes, I believe I remember seeing one."

"Excellent. Tromdel must have returned it after Faymia and I fled to the south," the man said. "Please come with me."

Dulnear and Son walked behind the ruined house to

the outbuilding. The wagon that Dulnear had been forced to tow to Shenndel's property had indeed been returned there, and the two of them began to pull it around to the front of the house.

As they worked together, Son told Dulnear all about his encounter with Searfain. When he reached the part about the man falling down the stairs and dying he hesitated, and looked away. "I didn't mean for him to die," he said with a tremble in his voice.

Dulnear swelled with sympathy. He knew the gentle boy's heart well. He stopped pulling, walked to Son, and bent down on one knee. Looking him in the eyes, he said, "I know that you did not. I do not believe that you would ever want anyone to die." A tear formed in the man's eye and he continued, "His own violent heart is what killed him. It was not you." He then pulled Son close and the boy wept. "Thank you for believing in me, Son," he said. "We are almost finished here, and then I will never return."

"Promise?" his young friend asked, wiping his nose on the sleeve of his coat.

"Promise," the man from the north said, wiping a tear from his own face.

"Okay," Son said as he regained his composure. "I'm ready."

When they reached the front of the house, Faymia was stirring. Dulnear went to her and asked, "How are you feeling?"

Still laying in the grass, the woman reached her hand toward her face, swallowed and answered, "My head is throbbing."

The man from the north looked at Son and instructed,

"There is a wild cherry tree that grows near the eastern garden. Gather as many cherries as you can. Eating those should help with the pain."

"Okay," Son said as he ran off toward the garden.

Dulnear fetched a canteen from Tapp's saddlebag and brought it to Faymia. He sat down beside her and she sat up to drink from it. "I am awfully sorry that you were injured," he said sincerely. "I should have been more cautious. Will you please forgive me?"

"It's not your fault," the woman said. "I insisted on coming, remember?"

Dulnear looked at his friend's face. The sight of her injured eye and the purple, swollen cheek broke his heart. "But I promised to do everything I could to protect you and the boy."

Faymia reached out and took his hand. She gave him a reassuring smile and said, "It's okay. You are still my champion and—"

Just then, Son ran up with his coat pockets stuffed with cherries. He knelt in front of Faymia and began piling them on the ground in front of her. "I got as many as I could carry. They're quite delicious! Would you like me to get some more?" he asked.

"That should be enough for now," Dulnear answered as he stood up. "I need you to hitch Mor to the cart."

"Okay," the boy said. "What are you going to do?"

Dulnear inhaled deeply and gazed at the burned-out house. He then answered, "I need to get something from in there."

Dulnear carefully stepped through the remains of his once great home. The roof had fallen in during the fire, and beams of pale light found their way through the wreckage. An eerie feeling possessed him as he looked around and viewed the mansion in its current dilapidated state. All that he owned was now in ruins, and it was burned by his own choice. It felt much like a strange dream to him. His surroundings were familiar, yet altogether foreign at the same time.

Stepping around black, smoldering floorboards that had fallen from the stories above, the man from the north made his way to the large fireplace located in what used to be the dining room. After moving some scorched furniture and a few large boards out of the way, he stood and looked at it for a while, examining the stones that formed the broad chimney.

He squatted down and looked inside the fireplace. He then withdrew a knife and used it to drag the two long, heavy andirons from the hearth without touching the hot metal. He examined the stones forming the fireplace and chimney one more time, feeling along their edges.

Finding a stone where the mortar had begun to crumble around it, Dulnear used the knife to chip away what remained until it came loose and could easily be removed. It was about the size of a loaf of bread, and he used it to break away the other stones that surrounded the new open space. Once enough was broken away, the opening of the fireplace became tall enough for him to crouch inside without too much difficulty.

He stood hunched inside the fireplace, feeling the stones at the back of it for more crumbling mortar.

Once he found a loose rock, he knocked it out of place, praying that the chimney would not come falling down around him.

Delicately removing stone after stone from the back of the fireplace, Dulnear opened up a hidden chamber that was barely deep and wide enough for the iron chest that was hidden inside of it. He used his knife to hook one of the handles of the chest and dragged it out into the open. Once he had it in a place with enough space and light, he knelt, checked to make sure it was not too hot, swallowed, and opened it.

Under the lid of the iron box was a fortune of gold and silver coins. As the man from the north ran his hand over it, he recalled the time his father told him about the treasure, and how he'd dreamed of all the ways he would spend the money when the time came for him to inherit it. Now, none of the things he wanted so badly during his youth seemed to hold any appeal to him. He only wanted to live in a way that was simple, and peaceful. Status and attention had become distasteful, for they had only ever brought him trouble.

Dulnear dragged the chest through the wreckage and out the door. The fresh air felt good in his lungs and removed the sting in his chest from the smoking debris. As he moved closer to the wagon, he could see Son and Faymia sitting in the grass together, and he called out, "Son, would you help me get this into the wagon?"

The boy jumped up and ran to the cart. Dulnear hefted one end of the chest onto it and strained to keep it from falling back to the ground. Son climbed inside and grabbed one of the still warm handles, pulling hard as his friend lifted and pushed from the other end.

Once the chest was in, they situated it at the front of the wagon. Dulnear then gave Son instructions to fetch a canvas tarp and a couple of boards from the outbuilding. When the boy returned with the items, they used them to hide the treasure.

"That box is incredibly heavy! What's in there?" Son asked.

Dulnear smiled and answered, "Her freedom," as he nodded toward the resting Faymia.

"So that chest is what we came here for?"

"Yes," the man from the north said. "It is an inheritance meant for me, my children, and their children."

Son's eyes grew big as he asked, "How much is in there?"

"I really do not know," Dulnear answered. "This chest has been in my family for generations. It has been hidden behind the fireplace since the house was built. When I was younger, I assumed that I would dig it up and spend it. But after my father died, I decided to leave it there for my descendants, just as he did for me. Now that we have it, we need to be leaving quickly."

"Okay," the boy said. "I noticed there was leather and some tools in the barn. Can I collect a few things before we go?"

"Of course," Dulnear said. "But please be swift about it. We must be leaving before anyone comes looking for Searfain."

The man from the north gently lifted Faymia from her resting place and laid her in the back of the wagon. His shoulder was still aching, and it was an awkward task to perform while wearing a sling, but he managed.

When Son returned, he stowed the leather and tools in his saddlebag and mounted Tapp. "Where are we going?" he asked.

"Ahmcathare," Dulnear answered. "It is time to have a visit with the slavers."

CHAPTER SIXTEEN
FOR FREEDOM'S SAKE

A DAY LATER, DULNEAR AND FAYMIA sat by the fire while Son was off catching dinner. It was a pleasant evening, and the ever-gray Aun sky was growing darker. "How do you feel?" the man asked.

"Much better," Faymia answered. She kept her gaze away from her friend, and the tone of her voice didn't seem to match her answer.

"Son did a fine job on your eyepatch," the man said, referring to the leather patch the boy made for her.

"Yes, he did," she said as she folded her arms and leaned in a little closer to the fire. "How is your shoulder?" she asked.

"Fine," he said, moving his right arm up and down. Then he smiled and said, "I think I am ready to wear the iron hand again."

Faymia's expression didn't change as she stared into the fire. Her shoulders drooped and her nose turned pink.

"Are you sure you are okay?" the man asked as he reached his left hand out to touch her shoulder.

A tear slowly ran down his friend's cheek. "I'm hideous," she said. "My face is scarred, and I have to wear a patch so that I don't frighten small children with my dead eye."

Dulnear moved closer and gently rubbed Faymia's back. He struggled to find comforting words. Eventually he came up with, "I find the eyepatch to be"—he paused for a moment, then continued—"alluring."

The woman froze, wrinkled her forehead, and looked at Dulnear with an expression of disbelief. "Did you just say, alluring?" she asked.

Dulnear swallowed hard. His face suddenly felt hot, and he hoped she was unable to see that he was turning red in the fading light. "Well, it is just that you look so strong, and you fought against a man many times your size..." He then trailed off as he mumbled something about marks of bravery and slowly, self-consciously, removed his hand from her back.

Faymia continued to look at the man from the north. Eventually, the corners of her mouth turned upward and a laugh escaped through her tense lips. Dulnear nervously laughed in return. He had hoped it was an appropriate response, but he really wasn't sure. Then, the woman began to laugh harder, and it set his mind at ease. She wrapped both of her arms around his arm and rested her head against his shoulder.

"You really do have a way with words," the injured runaway said, giggling.

The man from the north wasn't completely sure what had just transpired, but was glad that his friend seemed comforted.

Soon after, Son arrived with a rabbit for each of them. He skinned them and roasted them over the fire. As the three of them ate together, he asked, "How much longer until we reach Ahmcathare?"

"We should be there in about three days," the man from the north answered. "We will not be traveling all the way into Ahmcathare though. The tavern where Faymia once worked is in a town on the outskirts, and that is where we will be visiting."

As they spoke, Faymia's disposition changed again. The relaxed demeanor she'd held minutes before was gone, and she got up to dispose of the remains of their dinner.

"Will we be able to go into the city and spend some time there?" the boy asked, licking his fingers clean and rubbing them on the grass.

Dulnear watched Faymia as she busied herself. "I believe the wisest thing will be for us to return the horses to Aesef as quickly as possible. Perhaps we can visit Ahmcathare another time," he answered. He then stared into the fire as he rehearsed in his mind the transaction that was going to take place when they arrived at the tavern.

Faymia laid awake as the last flames of the fire flickered out. She couldn't get comfortable, as every stone and lump in the ground underneath her seemed more pronounced than usual. Dulnear was asleep nearby, breathing heavily. Son was also asleep, and a faint snore could be heard coming from his direction. Having both of them close brought her a sense of safety, but there were still thoughts that tugged at her mind, making it difficult for her to be at ease.

It felt like an extremely long time since she had

seen her former slaver, Tcharron, and she was nervous about what was going to happen when they arrived in Ahmcathare. He had always been harsh and belittling to her, and frequently reminded her that she existed solely for the pleasure of men and the profit of her slaver. There was something about him that made her feel powerless and of no account. She didn't like the person she was around him, and she dreaded the possibility of becoming that person again.

As she struggled to process thoughts of seeing the slaver once again, the events of the last several months played themselves over and over in her mind. She had felt hope, strength, terror, and pain, all in greater measure than ever before, and sometimes all at once. As she gently touched the leather patch over her eye, she thought about how freedom comes at a price, and that the greatest rewards in life often require the greatest risks. She had taken more risks since meeting the man from the north than she had taken in her entire life, and all of those risks were leading to whatever was going to happen the next day.

She also found herself concerned for the safety of her friends. The last time she'd encountered Tcharron, he'd had a group of Malitae with him, and they tried to kill Dulnear. She then thought to herself, *Why would he go through all of that trouble to recover a worthless slave?* It was a question that nagged at her until she was finally overtaken by a fitful, restless sleep.

"We will leave the cart and horses here," Dulnear explained as he directed Mor off of the road and into a clearing. It was mid-afternoon and they were close to the village, so it was difficult to find a place where the wagon would not be seen by other travelers. When he felt that they were a sufficient distance from the road, he halted the horse, climbed down from the cart, and retrieved a few things from Mor's saddlebag, including the iron fist.

Son and Faymia also dismounted and joined him. "What are we going to do?" the boy asked.

"I am going to make a business transaction," the man from the north answered. "But I need your help." He reached into his bag, produced several leather pouches, and handed them to Son. "Will you please fill these with gold and silver from the chest?"

The boy took the pouches and hopped into the cart. As he filled them, Dulnear rolled up his coat sleeve and began attaching the iron fist. Faymia walked closer to help and, as she buckled the leather straps, he looked at her face. There was something about her in that moment that seemed to cause everything else around them to fade until the only thing he saw clearly was her. It dawned on him that he was about to take a tremendous chance for her freedom, and a voice from inside of him asked, *Is she worth it?*

"Absolutely," the man from the north said out loud, though he was convinced that his answer was only in his mind.

"Absolutely what?" the woman asked as she finished securing the hand and pulled the fur sleeve back into place.

"Hmm? Oh, just thinking out loud," he said with a swallow.

"About what?" Faymia asked with an amused smile.

"You know. Different things." He could feel his ears turning red, and was about to say something else when Son came down from the cart hefting several full pouches.

"That's about half the chest!" the boy exclaimed.

"Thank you," Dulnear said as he began taking the bags and placing them in various pockets throughout his long fur coat. When he finished, the boy was still holding one leather pouch stuffed with coins. "I want you to hold onto that one," he explained. "You can keep it in Tapp's saddlebag."

"Why?" the boy asked.

"Because I want you to stay here and wait," Dulnear said. "If anyone other than myself or Faymia comes back here, ride off as fast as you can. There will be enough in your saddlebag to take care of you and Maren for some time, so do not try to save the chest. You will only lose what you already have in the process."

Son's shoulders dropped and he exhaled. "But I want to come with you," he protested.

The man from the north paused and smiled. "I know you do. You are the bravest lad in Aun," he said. "But this is not the time for a show of force. Besides, I need to know that, no matter what happens today, you will make it back to Aesef and Maren safely."

"Okay," the boy conceded.

Dulnear reached down and hugged Son, and Faymia did the same. "Pray," she said with a smile.

"I want you to wait for us on your horse," the man from the north instructed. "If we do not return by nightfall, then take the Cidens road toward Blackcloth until you reach Aesef's farm."

Son nodded in acknowledgement and gave his friend a final hug. He then mounted his horse and watched as they turned and began walking toward the road that led to the village.

When the tavern was in sight, Dulnear's stomach turned. The last time he was there, Tcharron's men attacked him, and he narrowly escaped by leaping out of a second-story window. It was not an occurrence he wished to repeat.

He and Faymia stepped into the bar. The slaver could be seen seated at a long table toward the back. His associates sat around him, drinking, and a Malitae warrior stood behind him. The southern fighter was the first to notice Dulnear and he drew a knife, then alerted Tcharron to the man's presence. Immediately, he whispered something to the other slavers and they all reached into their coats and vests for blades of various shapes and sizes.

Standing, Tcharron obnoxiously called out, "Well, if it isn't the enormous goat! Is that my slave with you?"

Dulnear approached the table with Faymia by his side. The smell of scented musk mixed with tavern smoke did little for his mood. He kept his cool and thought hard about what he was going to say next. "I am not here to fight with you, slaver," he said. "I came to make things right."

Tcharron gave a disgusted glare toward the woman's eyepatch. "You brought her back damaged," he complained. "How do you mean to make that right?"

The man from the north maintained eye contact with the slaver but observed the Malitae and his restless companions the best he could. He resisted the urge to

177

keep his hand close to his sword as he spoke. He also did his best to keep his iron fist hidden. "I intend to purchase her," he announced.

Tcharron raised an eyebrow and scratched his jaw. Looking Dulnear up and down, he said, "Purchase her? What do you mean by that?"

Dulnear tried to keep the sarcasm from his voice as he answered, "I would like to give you money in exchange for this slave."

The slaver shook his head, then glanced at the others at the table. With a caustic grin, he asked, "And what are you prepared to give me for this used-up runaway?"

The man from the north retrieved one of the leather pouches from the inside of his coat. It was more than enough to pay for multiple slaves. He set it on the table in front of Tcharron. "This should suffice," he said confidently.

Tcharron opened the pouch and examined its contents. His eyes grew wide for just a moment before his face turned serious. "Pursuing a runaway slave is expensive," he said. "And the Malitae do not work cheap. How do you plan to make that right?"

Dulnear produced another bag of coins and placed it on the table. "This should more than cover your expenses," he said. Then he placed a third leather pouch on the table and added, "And this is for your man that I killed. I deeply regret that. I hope this helps in making up for the loss"

Tcharron swallowed hard as he looked at the silver and gold in front of him. The men seated at the table stared greedily and whispered to each other. Finally, the slaver started to laugh. "I accept your payment for the old strumpet. You, however, are perhaps the dumbest man in all of Aun. On the night you came in here, you should have just walked away. She is not worth all of this."

The man from the north noticed that Faymia was hanging her head, trying to inconspicuously wipe a tear from her cheek. He looked at Tcharron squarely and exclaimed, "She is worth it to me."

"Very well," the slaver said. He whispered something to the man sitting next to him and he produced a parchment. After signing it, he said, "Here are her papers. She's yours to do with as you please."

Dulnear stuffed the scroll into his coat and gave a final stare toward Tcharron before nodding and turning toward the door. As he and Faymia were stepping out of the pub, he could hear the group of men explode in raucous laughter. He gritted his teeth and continued out into the street, resisting any temptation to give the slavers what they deserved.

When the two of them were several paces down the road and away from the tavern, a voice called out, "Northerner!"

Dulnear peered back and was surprised to see the Malitae warrior standing in the street. His muscles tensed, and he stepped in front of Faymia. "What do you want?" he called back.

As the southern warrior approached him, the man from the north could see that he was carrying a familiar weapon. The Malitae handed him a large sword. It was the one he had used for most of his life. He had lost it in the Fuar River and believed he would never see it again. His mouth fell open and he uttered, "Thank you. How did you recover it?"

The man said nothing in response to the question. Without expression, he turned around and began walking the way he came. Dulnear watched him and, to his surprise, he didn't return to the tavern. Instead, he continued to walk south until he was out of sight.

Dulnear and Faymia were out of the village and almost to the clearing where Son was waiting. The man from the north stopped in the road and placed his hand on his friend's shoulder. "How are you faring?" he asked.

The woman swallowed and looked up at him. "I feel strange," she said. "I fear that I am going to wake up and discover that all of this is a dream."

"This is very real," Dulnear assured her. He then pulled the slave papers from his coat and opened them. After quickly reading them over, he rolled them up and handed them to her. He also gave her one of the pouches of gold coins. "You are free, Faymia. No man owns you, and you can do anything your heart desires."

The woman grasped her cloak just below her neck and gasped, "I don't know what to say! It's been so long. I owe you my life."

"You owe me nothing," the man answered. "If not for you, I would have died on the road to Blackcloth. You have saved my life in more ways than one."

"But," Faymia stammered, "what my heart desires most, more than anything, is to be with you."

Dulnear's stomach felt funny, and he felt a strange

tingling on his skin. "I would like that very much. But not because you feel obligated or—"

"I love you," the woman interrupted. She then blushed deep pink and looked down.

The man from the north froze. His heart was warm and happy. Finally, he drew closer to his friend, lifted her chin, and kissed her lovely, soft lips. Their kiss became an embrace, and he lifted her off the ground as they wrapped their arms around each other. "And I you," he said before gently returning her to the ground.

The two stood there, looking into each other's eyes. "How could you love someone like me?" Faymia asked.

Dulnear smiled and thought for a moment. "As I told you before, I have very high standards," he answered.

The woman returned his smile and hugged him again. "You are my Layoak," she said with a smile.

"Layoak? How do you know that word?" the man asked. "It is northern speak for hero."

"Aesef taught it to me," she said. "And that is what you are."

Dulnear chuckled. "Well, this Layoak is ready to go home," he said, and the two of them made their way back to the waiting Son and their horses.

CHAPTER SEVENTEEN
The Dance

ULNEAR, FAYMIA, AND SON RODE up to Aesef's house to find Maren sitting on the donkey with a book. "They're back!" she yelled before sliding off the animal and running inside, slamming the door behind her.

The three travelers looked at each other. "I guess she went to find Aesef," Son observed as he dismounted his horse and began to unfasten his saddlebag.

Dulnear and Faymia came down from the wagon. As they were gathering their things, the door of the house swung open. Maren had Aesef by the hand, pulling him outside with all of her might. "I'm coming!" the farmer assured her as they rushed to welcome their friends.

The man from the north knelt on one knee and the young girl threw herself into his arms. "It is wonderful to see you again!" he exclaimed as she squeezed his neck tightly.

Maren leaned back and looked the man over. "You still have a metal hand," she said.

"Yes, I do. I do not believe I will be getting my old one back," he replied with a grin.

"Did you smash things?" she asked, swinging her fist.

"Yes, I did," he answered. "It is very good for that."

"Good!" she said, and ran over to Faymia, who crouched down to hug her. After gripping the woman tightly, she looked intently at her eyepatch. She gently touched the edges of it and asked, "What happened to your eye?"

"It was injured in Tuas-arum," the woman answered. "Son made this patch for me."

Maren smiled widely and declared, "It's neat!" She then ran to the boy and cried, "Son!"

The boy picked Maren up and she wrapped her arms and legs around him as he held her tight. "I missed you," he said.

"I missed you," she returned. "Aesef gave me a new book."

"Do you like it?" the boy asked.

"Uh huh," she replied as she rested her head on his shoulder. "It's about pirates and magic ships."

"I'm glad," he said. "I can't wait for you to tell me all about it."

"Okay," she said, then paused for a moment. "Son?"

"Yes?"

"Could you make me an eyepatch like Faymia's?"

"Of course," he said with a chuckle, and set the girl down.

Aesef walked over and embraced the man from the north. His nose was red, and he looked as if he had been holding back tears. "I'm relieved to see you," he said.

"It is finished," Dulnear replied.

"All of it?"

"Yes, Faymia is free now. My home is with her and the children."

The tear that Aesef had been trying to hold back escaped, and he smiled so wide that it looked like it would never fade. "Praise the Great Father!" he exclaimed. "Maren and I prayed for you every night."

"Thank you," Dulnear said.

Aesef then hugged Faymia and asked, "How does it feel?"

The woman teared up as she looked beyond the farmer in thought. "It's going to take some getting used to but it's wonderful beyond words."

"And so are you," the old man said. He then turned toward Son. "And you, loyal young champion, how was your journey?"

"Dulnear had a mansion," he answered. "I've never seen anything like it. Then he burned it down"

The farmer's eyebrows shot up. "Burned it down, eh? I suppose that's one way to keep your eyes on the road ahead of you," he said. "I'll bet you didn't know that your friend was a nobleman, did you?"

"I guess not," the boy said.

"Never judge a book by its furry cover," Aesef said, laughing. "And don't worry about the house. Mansions do not make one noble. Acts of sacrifice, like the ones Dulnear made, are more noble than all the land and wealth in Aun."

The old man then turned his attention back toward Dulnear. "How did Tapp and Mor do for you?" he asked.

"They are exceptional beasts," the man from the north answered. "Strong and swift."

"Good. I want you to keep them," the farmer said.

Dulnear's eyes widened as he protested, "I cannot take your horses. I am just as happy on my feet."

"I insist," Aesef said. "It is a long walk to Laor, and you can use them on your farm."

Conceding, the warrior answered, "I could never repay you for all of your kindness."

"It is completely my pleasure," his friend beamed.

Dulnear's demeanor then suddenly shifted. His mouth became dry, and he scraped his hand through his hair. He lowered his voice and said, "Before you offered me the horses, I was going to ask a favor of you."

"Anything, my friend," the farmer said.

The man's voice got even quieter, and he leaned in so no one else could hear. "I would like to have a wedding before returning to Laor."

"A wedding?" the farmer said as he jerked his head back.

"Yes," the man from the north said as he swallowed, trying to return some moisture to his mouth. "I intend to ask Faymia for her hand in marriage."

"When?"

"Tonight," he answered. "After dinner."

Aesef smiled thoughtfully and rubbed his chin. "I know a friar, and I can have Phel prepare the barn. Does that sound adequate?"

"More than adequate," Dulnear answered. "You are a true friend."

"One question. Do you have a ring?" the farmer asked.

The man from the north raised an eyebrow and discreetly produced a ring from his coat pocket. "It was my mother's," he explained.

Aesef quietly chuckled, "It's a bit large for her wee finger. Don't you think?"

"I suppose you are right," Dulnear said. "Perhaps I can place it on her big toe."

"You just keep that in a safe place," the farmer laughed. "I think I have just the thing."

Dulnear smiled in appreciation, realizing the absurdity of his idea. "Thank you," he said. "I am just a bit nervous. I am not very knowledgeable about the ways of love."

"It is indeed a lifelong education," Aesef said. "But I think you're off to a good start."

After dinner, Dulnear and Faymia slipped outside while the others tidied up. An unusually warm breeze gently blew over them, carrying the scent of nearby wildflowers. They walked away from the house together but didn't go far, since the light from the inside was the only thing keeping their surroundings from being completely dark.

"I think Maren is quite taken with you," the man from the north observed.

"She's lovely," Faymia said, smiling. "Quirky and honest."

Dulnear chuckled, "That, in part, is the graymind. I do not believe she is capable of being dishonest about her opinions. I hope you did not take offense to her eyepatch."

"None at all," the woman said. "She looks adorable in it, and she plays a proper pirate."

"I agree," the man said. He continued to make small talk, trying to find a natural way to transition to the question of marriage. "So, are you looking forward to journeying to Laor?"

"I'm a bit weary from traveling," she answered honestly, "but I am looking forward to seeing where you and the children live."

Dulnear realized that the moment he had at present was probably going to be the best he was going to get. His left hand was sweaty, and he wiped it on his coat before taking Faymia's hand. They stopped walking and he looked at her. As he did, the whole earth seemed to be spinning around him and a strange dizziness threatened to disrupt his footing. Her face was lovely, but seemed to move closer and further away as he looked at it. "Are you okay?" she asked.

"Yes. Why do you ask?" he said, squinting in a peculiar manner.

"It's just that you look ill," she said.

It dawned on Dulnear that his expression may have given away the nervousness he felt, and he now wished that he would have walked her further into the darkness before taking her hand. He tried to swallow but his mouth refused to cooperate. He cleared his thoughts and began, "Faymia, you know that I love you. You are dearer to me than you will ever know. You are my Elayainn, the warmth in my heart. Will you travel to Laor with me as my bride?"

Faymia smiled. All of the lines she normally wore on her face seemed to disappear, and a tear slowly made its way down her lovely face. "Oh, my Layoak, you know that I will," she said.

The two stood and stared at each other for quite some time. Finally, Dulnear remembered something. "Oh, I almost forgot," he said. Then he knelt on one knee and took a ring from his pocket.

Faymia's eyes lit up and she held out her hand as her friend placed the ring on her finger. "It's beautiful!" she exclaimed. "Where did it come from?"

"It belonged to Aesef," the man from the north explained. "His love wore it, and he wanted us to have it." He then stood and hugged Faymia. "I am so grateful for you!" he exclaimed.

"And I you," the woman gushed.

Suddenly, a small voice could be heard calling out from the house. "Hey! Have you done it yet?" Maren shouted, wearing an eyepatch identical to Faymia's.

The couple laughed and Dulnear called back, "Yes, I did it."

"Yessss!" the girl celebrated, and she ran out to join them.

Not far behind were Son and Aesef. "Great going!" Son cheered as he hugged his warrior friend. He then turned and hugged Faymia. "I'm so happy for you both," he said, beaming.

"Congratulations," the old farmer said to Dulnear. "All of the adventures you've had until now are nothing compared to what lies ahead."

"I believe that to be true," the warrior said. "But I am ready."

The five of them celebrated the engagement long into the night. As they shared stories and made plans for the wedding, all of the trials and struggles of the previous months seemed to be forgotten, replaced by the kind of lightness that one wishes would last forever.

The inside of the barn could scarcely be recognized. Phel and the other farmhands had turned it into a beautiful chapel. Flowers were transformed into strings of garland that hung from the ceiling, chairs were brought from inside of the house, and tall candelabras, with candles burning bright, lined either side of an aisle that ran down the center of the makeshift church.

The seats were full, and Son, Maren, and Aesef were situated in the front row, dressed in formal clothing that the old farmer had provided. As the bride and groom made their way down the aisle, young Maren pointed to the crown of flowers on Faymia's head and whispered to Son, "Those are just like mine!"

After their walk down the aisle, a young friar stood with Dulnear and Faymia under a beautiful arch made of wild twigs and flowers. He nervously cleared his throat and began to read from his book of liturgies. His hands shook so badly that he often lost his place and had to repeat himself as he searched for the last sentence he'd read. With sweat running down his temples, he continued, "Lord Dulnear, do you have anything you would like to say to the Lady Faymia?"

The man from the north suppressed a smile. He wasn't accustomed to being called lord, and he was entertained by the nervous, wobbly friar. He looked at his bride and noticed that she also had an amused smile forming across her lips. Finally, he spoke. "My Elayainn, you have my sword, my heart, my strength, and my undying

189

commitment. I am arrested by your beauty, your passion, your kindness, and your love, and I am yours forever."

The friar wiped a tear from his eye, then swallowed. "And you, Lady Faymia, do you have words?"

The woman smiled and gazed into the eyes of her groom as she said, "My wonderful Layoak. You have set me free in so many ways, and I am profoundly grateful that you are in my life. I give my love, my affection, my devotion, and my years to you and only you."

The friar then wiped another tear from his eye, sniffled, and announced, "Inasmuch as the Lord Dulnear and Lady Faymia have pledged their troth to be married this day, we call upon the Great Father to bless this union." He then continued nervously, "If anyone can show just cause why they may not be joined together, let them now speak, or else hereafter keep silent for all time." He then cleared his throat and added, "Also, if you have an objection, Lord Dulnear will be waiting for you outside with his sword."

The crowd erupted with laughter at the friar's statement until the man from the north turned to them and said sternly, "I mean it." He then winked and gave a playful grin before turning back to the nervous minister.

With trembling hands, the friar then tied a cord around the bride and groom's joined hands. "By this cord you are now and forevermore bound to each other," he said. "Lord Dulnear, you may kiss your bride."

The man from the north shook the cord from his hand, lifted the woman off of her feet, closed his eyes, and kissed her full on the lips. As he did, he drank in the softness, the scent, and the taste of their first kiss as husband and wife.

It was a strange and wonderful sensation that lingered with him for a long time to come.

When Dulnear set Faymia back down on her feet, the friar had them face their friends as he announced, "By the power vested in me, I now pronounce you husband and wife."

Cheers and applause rose up, and those in attendance lined up to congratulate them, many of them leaving gifts or coins at their feet. The barn was rearranged as tables filled with steaming lamb, vegetables, pies, and cakes were brought in.

Musicians played and, as they did, Son and Maren joined Dulnear and Faymia for a dance of celebration. Swinging, twirling, and swaying, they celebrated their new life together, often sharing dreams and thoughts about their home in Laor, and gushing with congratulations and words of gratitude. It was the grandest time any of them had ever experienced, and one they would never forget.

CHAPTER EIGHTEEN
HOME

THE JOURNEY TO LAOR WAS uneventful, though it could have taken much less time if Maren hadn't insisted on taking Earl with them. The mule seemed to be in a constant state of hunger, slowing their journey as it stopped to nibble on the lush grass that grew alongside the road. Most of the time, the young girl was so engrossed in her book that she didn't bother to goad the animal on when it stopped to snack. Somewhere along the journey, she removed the eyepatch that Son had made for her and placed it on the donkey, who didn't seem to mind wearing it at all.

When they finally arrived, Dulnear halted his horse on the road and looked out over the farm. A feeling came over him that reassured him that he was home. It was a sense that all was well, and he paused silently for a moment to take it in and be grateful.

"It's a bit grown over," Son broke in, pointing out to the garden. "I'll have to get to work on it tomorrow."

Still gazing over the humble property, the man from the north said quietly, "It is perfect." Then he turned toward Son and said with a smile, "It is good to be home."

After making a space for the horses in the barn, Son showed Dulnear and Faymia the toys he had been making, and made sure the woman had a sufficient tour of the house. Afterward, they enjoyed a modest meal together and discussed plans to build a pen for the animals.

That night, it felt good for the man from the north to be able to lie down on the bed he had built before returning to Tuas-arum. It was the only bed in southern Aun that fit him properly, and there was still room for Faymia. Though a chill hung in the night air, he slept soundly with his bride curled up beside him. "You are all elbows and knees," he told her at bedtime, but he really didn't mind at all.

As he slept, Dulnear dreamed he was floating far off of the ground. Looking down, he could see the burned, blackened wreckage of his estate. Feelings of disdain toward the violent, unreasoning, impaired culture of his people rose up inside of him. Any desire to return to the place of his upbringing had completely left him.

Suddenly, he found himself hovering over the home of Shenndel. He could see the bloodstained tree stump where his hand was removed, and he was humbled to tears. He saw the old man standing there, bitter, lonely, and far from any real peace. Thorndel's father was a shell of a man, alive only in the sense that his heart still beat and there was breath in his lungs. He knew that he would have been destined for the same fate, had he not left his home and journeyed south to find a better way.

The dreaming man from the north took a deep breath, rose higher into the sky, and flew away south. He felt lighter and happier than he had ever felt before. Though it was only a dream, the joy and cheer in his heart were as real as anything in the waking world. Every weight had lifted, every regret cast off, and every tie to what once was had been severed. He was free.

I hope you enjoyed reading *Man from the North*. Its characters and their adventures are near and dear to me. If you would like information about my next fantasy book, *Daughter of Two Worlds*, as well as other forthcoming projects, please visit my website at www.leebezotte.com and sign up for my e-newsletter.

Thank you for journeying with me!
Lee Bezotte